TOWING THE LINE

NICOLA MARSH

I need a new start. Anonymity. In a country where no one will know me, and the havoc I create.

Not all the rumors about me are true. But I made one mistake too many in LA and attending an Australian college for a few semesters is the perfect solution.
I plan on avoiding guys. But the part-time tutor and sexy Aussie artist Ashton? Has me re-evaluating the wisdom of being a reformed bad girl.

Ash is aloof, dedicated, serious, and I must corrupt him. So I seduce him. Not expecting to fall in love for the first time. And the last.

Because Ash has high standards and when he learns the truth about me, he'll join the long list of people in my life pretending I don't exist.

AUTHOR'S NOTE:

Grammatically, 'toeing the line' is correct.

But in Dani's story, the mistakes of her past are holding her back. She feels like she's dragging an invisible weight behind her, hence 'towing the line'.

Copyright © Nicola Marsh 2014
Published by Nicola Marsh 2014

All the characters in this book have no existence outside the imagination of the author and have no relation whatsoever to anyone bearing the same name or names. They're not distantly inspired by any individual known or unknown to the author and all the incidents in the book are pure invention.

All rights reserved including the right of reproduction in any form. The text or any part of the publication may not be reproduced or transmitted in any form without the written permission of the publisher.

The author acknowledges the copyrighted or trademarked status and trademark owners of the word marks mentioned in this work of fiction.

ONE
DANI

"Where's Loverboy?"

Not that I really cared where Mia's boyfriend Kye was. I was enjoying having my BFF all to myself for a few hours before I boarded a plane to Australia to start my new life.

"He'll be here soon," Mia said, shoving the half-empty pizza box in my direction. "Said he had to see a man about a dog."

I helped myself to another slice of pepperoni, even though I'd barely nibbled the first. "What the hell does that mean?"

Mia shrugged. "Who knows? I just nod and smile when he comes out with those indecipherable Aussie-isms." Her eyes lit up. "Besides, who cares when he's that cute?"

"Fair enough," I said, eternally grateful we could actually talk like this considering I'd recently fucked up majorly by coming onto Kye with the intention of deliberately hurting Mia.

I'd been acting like the attention-seeking idiot I was and thankfully, Mia and Kye had forgiven me.

I'd told Mia the truth. Well, most of it.

She knew about the baby, why I'd blown off college and why I'd spent the last three years drifting through a haze of partying to forget.

But she didn't know all of it.

Nobody did.

And I intended on keeping it that way.

Sensing my sudden reticence, Mia pushed her plate away and placed a hand on my arm. "You okay?"

I nodded, swallowing the unexpected lump of emotion in my throat. I never got sentimental. Ever. I'd given up being that vulnerable a long time ago. Because feelings led to pain and I never wanted to feel as bad as I did when that bitch of a nurse told me I'd 'lost' my baby.

Like I'd lose anything so precious.

"Guess the reality of leaving all this to attend college in Melbourne for a while has finally hit home." I gestured at the lavish lounge in my parents' Beverly Hills mansion. "I mean, how will I live without the ten widescreens, daily fresh sushi and thousand-thread count toilet paper?"

Mia laughed. "I hear they have two-thousand thread count in Australia." She winked. "How do you think Aussie guys have such hot asses?"

I chuckled, relieved the urge to bawl had receded.

"Talking about me?" Kye Sheldon strode into the room. Tall, blue-eyed, broad-shouldered, he was seriously hot and only had eyes for Mia as he made a beeline for his girlfriend and laid a hot, open-mouthed kiss on her right in front of me.

"Get a room," I muttered, actually enjoying the sight of my best friend being cherished in the way she deserved.

And Mia did deserve it. She'd always been good and why she'd hung out with me for the last fifteen years was beyond me. She was loyal, sweet and trusting. My voice of reason, I'd always called her. Which is why I hadn't told her about the baby.

Because when it came down to it, when I'd fallen pregnant at eighteen, I hadn't wanted to hear all the logical reasons why I shouldn't keep the baby. For the first time in my life, I would've had someone in my life to love me unconditionally. Someone to depend on me. Someone whose world revolved around me.

I'd never had that before. My parents pretended like their only child didn't exist. Too busy living an A-list Hollywood lifestyle in their suck-up job as agents to the stars.

Friends? Non-existent, discounting Mia, who had lived next door until her dad quit professional tennis to open his teaching academy in Santa Monica, and they'd moved. Mia had been my rock for so long. And I'd almost lost her through my own stupidity.

It had been the wake-up call I'd needed.

Time to stop drifting through life filled with self-pity. Time to make a new start. Time to start living again.

"Sorry," Kye drawled, not sounding sorry in the least as he sat next to Mia, his arm draped across her shoulders as she snuggled into him. "So Dani, ready to find a hot Aussie of your own Down Under?" He smirked. "Guys in Melbourne won't know what hits them when they get a squiz at you."

"Squiz?" I wrinkled my nose. "I'm hoping that's a good thing."

He chuckled. "Means a look at you."

Mia tweaked his nose. "Isn't he adorable?"

I rolled my eyes. "You two are pathetic."

"It's luuuurv," Kye said, holding Mia tighter. "So how about it? Ready to take Melbourne by storm?"

"Academically, maybe." Because that was my number

one priority. To make the most of the six months exchange program I'd been offered at the prestigious Melbourne University and start an Arts major. Thanks to Kye's dad pulling strings at the university, I had a chance at a new life. I wouldn't screw it up this time. "I can't thank your dad enough for this opportunity."

"He's the best." The visible pride in Kye's eyes made me well up again. Wish I had parents who cared enough about me to want to help my friends. "If you need anything while you're in Oz, don't hesitate to ring him."

I nodded. "That's what he told me when I Skyped him to say thanks for doing all this."

"He's a good guy." Kye's grin alerted me to another of his typical teasing barbs. "Speaking of guys—"

"Not interested." I held up my hand. "Even if you're personally acquainted with Jesse Spencer, Josh Helman and Ryan Kwanten, I don't care." I placed a hand over my heart. "I'm swearing off guys, even hot Aussie ones, for the next six months."

Mia gazed adoringly at Kye. "Never say never, sweetie." She pecked Kye on the cheek. "Trust me, there's something about Aussie guys that is irresistible."

"I'll take your word for it," I said, meaning it.

I'd spent the last three years hanging out with the wrong guys, sleeping with some of them, getting wasted, doing whatever it took to forget my fucked up life.

The next six months in Australia? My own personal detox program.

No partying, no drinking, no drugs and no men.

Mia, ever perceptive, must've picked up on something in my expression, because she turned to Kye and said, "I'd love an orange soda."

"Coming right up." He stood and glanced at me. "Anything for you, Dani?"

I shook my head. "No thanks, I'm fine."

Biggest lie ever.

"No worries, back in a sec." He strolled toward the monstrous kitchen that included a breakfast nook complete with the latest video game consoles my dad loved. Kye would be a while. Last time he'd been here and volunteered to get us sodas, we'd found him playing some warrior shoot-out game an hour later.

The moment he left the room, Mia fixed me with a narrow-eyed stare. "You're in a funk and it's more than just living overseas for six months."

I sighed, wishing I could fob her off, but so tired of living a lie let alone telling another. "I'm terrified that even after doing all this, nothing will change and I'll still be the same screwed-up little girl screaming for attention."

Voicing my greatest fear didn't make me feel better. It made me feel sick to my stomach.

Because it was true. What if after all this I couldn't change? I couldn't forget? I couldn't learn to live with the mistakes of my past?

"Oh honey." Mia leaped off the sofa to come sit beside me on the floor. "You're the bravest person I know."

She took both my hands and wouldn't let go when I tried to extricate them. "It takes real guts to do what you're doing. Moving halfway across the world, making a start on a college degree, changing your lifestyle."

She squeezed my hands. "You've been through hell and you've made it through. This is your chance. And I have no doubt whatsoever you'll make the most of every exciting new minute."

"Will you be resurrecting your old pom-poms to go with that cheerleading routine?"

She laughed at my droll response. "You're going to be fine. Better than fine." She released my hands to pull me into a hug. "You're going to kick some serious Aussie ass."

Wish I had half her confidence because the way I was feeling now? Like I was standing on a precipice, about to go over the edge, with no safety net in sight.

TWO
ASHTON

I knew Mum was having a bad day the moment I neared her room and heard her grunts of frustration.

She'd always loved crossword puzzles but the more her brain deteriorated, the harder it became for her to do the simplest tasks, let alone find a three letter word for an Australian native bird.

I'd almost reached the end of the long corridor when a nurse laid a hand on my shoulder.

"Got a minute, Ashton?"

I stopped, turned and held my breath. Whenever one of the nurses wanted to talk before I visited Mum, it wasn't good.

"Hey Pam. How are you?"

"Good, thanks." The fifty-something redhead had the kindest eyes I'd ever seen. Pale blue eyes that were currently filled with concern. "But I wanted to have a quick word with you today."

The inevitable tension built in my temples and I quashed the urge to rub them. "Mum's okay?"

A pointless, dumb-arse question, considering Mum

hadn't been okay in a long time. Not since I'd checked her into this special accommodation home two years earlier because it had become untenable to care for her at home.

The official diagnosis? Early onset dementia courtesy of a long-term alcohol abuse problem.

My diagnosis? She'd partied too hard, done too many drugs and drunk her life into oblivion to obscure whatever demons dogged her as a washed-up B-grade actress.

I resented her lifestyle. I resented every shitty thing that resulted in her being here at the age of sixty-three.

"Judy had a rough night." Pam hesitated, before fixing me with a pitying stare. "She may not know you today."

Fuck.

We'd reached this stage already?

I'd been warned there'd be more days like this. That as the dementia progressed, Mum's memory would deteriorate to the point she'd consider me a stranger.

I hadn't expected it to happen so soon and no way in hell I was prepared to handle it.

"Okay, thanks," I said, hoping Pam didn't hear the hitch in my voice.

Not for the first time since Mum had been diagnosed, I wanted to crumple in a heap on the floor and cry like a baby. But considering I'd been the only man in this family for a long time, losing my shit wasn't an option.

I had to stand tall and do what had to be done. And that included ensuring I made enough money to pay for Mum's bills. Something that was becoming increasingly difficult to do as my commissions dried up.

I needed to keep painting. I needed to keep tutoring at the university. And I needed to stop feeling like I was an automaton, oblivious to everything but getting through each day.

It was affecting my art, this emptiness inside me. But I needed to quash emotions and stay cold inside because if I started to feel again, I'd break down for sure.

Despite her lifestyle and her failings, Mum had always done right by me. I had to do the same for her.

"You're a good son." Pam squeezed my arm. "Come find me later if you have any questions or just want to talk, okay?"

"Thanks."

I knew I wouldn't take Pam up on her offer. I could barely hold my shit together when I left here after my bi-weekly visits. No way could I face Pam's kindness, especially if Mum was as bad as expected today.

I took several deep breaths to clear the buzzing in my head and waited until I could muster a halfway normal expression, before knocking on Mum's door and entering.

"How's the crossword coming along?"

My heart twisted as her head lifted and our gazes locked. Mine deliberately upbeat. Hers eerily blank.

"Who the fuck are you?"

And with those five words, I almost lost it.

My hands shook so I stuffed them into my jacket pockets as I cautiously crossed the room to sit in an armchair opposite hers.

Keep it simple, the nurses had warned if this happened. Don't startle her or press her to remember. Be casual. As for the swearing, aggression was a common reaction in progressive dementia. But to hear the F bomb tumble from Mum's lips was as foreign to me as seeing her sitting in a pink toweling bathrobe at five in the afternoon.

She'd always been glamorous, dressed to the nines with perfect make-up from the time she rose to the time she came home from whatever party she'd attended. Even as a kid, I had memories of Mum's vivid red lipstick and strawberry-scented shampoo as she kissed me goodbye before heading to an audition, her high heels clacking on our wooden floorboards as she left me in the care of the teenager next door.

That glamorous woman was nowhere to be seen now. Her blonde hair had faded to a washed out yellowy-grey. Her brown eyes were ringed with lines and underscored by dark circles. Her shoulders were shrunken, her back curved, her muscles flaccid from lack of use.

My beautiful, exceptional mother was broken. An empty shell.

And it killed me a little bit more every time I visited.

"I'm Ashton," I said, wishing I could elaborate, wishing I could yell, 'I'm your son. The one who wiped the vomit off your face more times than I can count. Who found you passed out on the floor and carried you to bed countless times over the years. Who would do anything to have you back.'

But I said none of those things. Instead, I swallowed my resentment—at the lifestyle that had put her here—and forced a smile. "I see you're a fan of crosswords."

"Stupid bloody things." She picked up the pen she'd discarded and tapped it against the magazine. "Can you think of a five letter word for a boy's building toy?"

"Block," I said, remembering the toy sets she used to buy me when she scored a role.

I'd treasured every single one, taking my time constructing the blocks into elaborate houses or fire-stations or castles, knowing it could be a long time between jobs for Mum.

Not that she didn't try hard but she never quite cracked it for a starring role. She'd got by with TV commercials and bit parts in anything from soap operas to local feature films.

Having me at forty had changed her life.

Roles were scarce for aging actresses, especially pregnant ones. I often wondered if that had been the start of her downward spiral. If she blamed me for ruining her life.

If she did, she never showed it. Mum adored me, loving me to the point of smothering. And even as she deteriorated, partying harder to forget the fact she wasn't working much, I always came home to dinner on the table.

"Thanks." She scrawled the letters into the boxes, her hand shaky. "Could you help me do the rest?"

"Sure," I said, taking care not to startle her as I cautiously edged my chair next to hers. "I like crosswords."

Knowing I was pushing my luck, I added, "I used to do them with my Mum."

I waited, held my breath, hoping for some sign she knew who I was.

"She must be a lucky lady to have a son like you," she said, her smile wobbly as she glanced at me with those blank eyes that broke my heart.

"I'm the lucky one," I said, as I settled in to spend some time with my Mum, hoping I had the strength to do this.

Because the way I was feeling now? As brittle as tinder-dry bark, ready to snap and fly away on the slightest breeze.

I had to be stronger. Strong enough for the both of us.

THREE
DANI

Melbourne wasn't so bad. Not that I'd seen much of it beyond the freeway ride from the airport to Parkville, where the university was situated.

I had the impression of gardens, lots of gardens, amid the high-rise apartments and trendy terrace houses rimming the CBD. It was pretty, in a low-key glam kind of way. And the air was a hell of a lot more breathable than LA's.

The cab driver had dropped me off a few blocks from the university, outside a tidy row of small apartments, and I glanced at the address I'd typed into my cell to make sure I was at the right place.

This all seemed so ... quaint. Like I had stepped into someone else's life.

I didn't do quaint. I did bold and brash. I did loud rock and small pills. I did bad boys and good booze.

Not anymore, as I shouldered my backpack and dragged my wheelie suitcase up the short path to knock on the door.

Annabelle, the exchange student who'd be heading to Denver tomorrow to do her stint at DU for six months, had gushed in the emails we'd exchanged.

She'd been nauseatingly bubbly, the type of girl I'd despise on sight. Thank God we wouldn't be roomies, and I'd be renting her apartment instead.

When the door opened, I braced myself.

"Omigod, you must be Dani," the tiny redhead squealed. "Come in, come in." She waved her hands around like she was shooing away birds. "I'm so glad you're here."

That made one of us. I'd be a lot gladder when she left for the US.

I wasn't here to make friends. I was here to kick off my major as a jaded twenty-one year old student and get my shit together, not necessarily in that order.

"You're Annabelle?"

She giggled and all but dragged the backpack off me. "'Course. Sorry. I'm just so excited to meet you."

"Why?" I blurted out, regretting my incredulous tone when some of the enthusiasm in her big, blue eyes dimmed, like I'd just kicked a puppy.

"Because I'm shit-scared of heading to America for the first time and I need to pick your brains."

I laughed at her blunt honesty. "As long as I get the lowdown on life in Melbourne."

Annabelle grinned. "Deal." She pointed to a door on the left. "That's the main bedroom. Dump your stuff in there. I'm crashing at my folks tonight."

Relieved I wouldn't have to put up with her excessive exuberance for much longer, I headed toward the bedroom. "Thanks."

"When you're done, meet me in the kitchen for the grand tour." She made those annoying cutesy inverted comma signs with her fingers when she said grand tour. Like any idiot couldn't see this place was barely bigger than a postage stamp. "Tea? Coffee?"

I bit back my first response—vodka, straight up. "Black coffee. No sugar, please."

"Coming right up." She practically bounced into the kitchen and I sighed, exhausted to my bones.

Could be jetlag but I knew better. Seeing someone as bright and bubbly as Annabelle rammed home what I already knew: I was burned-out. Cynical. With an extremely low tolerance for bullshit.

Meeting a girl my age that still had stars in her eyes made me feel ancient. And sad in a way I hadn't imagined.

Was this what it would be like being an older student? Having to hang out with eternal optimists? God, I hoped not. I'd be on the first plane back to LA and into my favorite dive bar doing tequila shots before I could blink.

"Hurry up, Dani, I want to hear everything before I leave."

I winced at Annabelle's shout from the kitchen and dragged my ass along with my bags into the main bedroom.

The moment I stepped into the room, I wondered if the local souvenir shop had thrown up in here.

There was Aussie paraphernalia … everywhere.

Stuffed toy kangaroos of various sizes strewn across the bed, covered in a flag quilt. Tiny koalas clipped onto the wrought iron bed-head. Postcards from oddly named places like Mount Buggery, Poowong, Yorkeys Knob and Wonglepong pinned to a massive corkboard covering one wall.

And that was before I even spied the desk, stacked high with Lonely Planet guides and maps and 'what to do in Melbourne' magazines. Even the pencil holder was in the shape of a platypus, right next to the echidna eraser; weird animals I'd only ever seen on TV.

Oh boy.

Either Annabelle was a nut-job patriot or she'd done all this to welcome me.

I dabbed at my eyes, touched by the thought of a stranger going to this much trouble for me.

My parents had barely acknowledged my departure, let alone questioned why I was starting college at the ripe old age of twenty-one. Guess I should be grateful they'd handed me a new platinum AMEX as a bon voyage gift. 'Much easier to throw money at the problem', I'd overheard them say when I was sixteen and demanding a new Mustang.

It had been their parenting motto from the outset. Pay nannies to raise me. Buy me the best of everything, including friends, by throwing fabulous parties. Keep my pocket money flowing so I'd be wrapped up in the latest electronic gadget and wouldn't request their presence at sporting events or presentation evenings.

I lived in the same house as my parents but we didn't know each other at all.

They didn't care when I dropped out of college before I'd even started. They didn't care whether I came home at midnight or five AM. They didn't care, period.

Which only exacerbated the guilt I'd felt at the time for losing my baby: had I inherited an ounce of their apathy? Was it genetic? Was that why my baby died at twelve weeks?

"Fuck," I muttered, knuckling my eyes and taking several deep breaths before heading to the kitchen to face Annabelle.

She beamed as I entered. "Did you like it?"

Guess that answered the question of whether she'd deliberately decorated the bedroom for me.

I forced a smile. "It's great. Thanks."

She shrugged. "A couple of my mates throw massive

Australia Day parties every year so they had a lot of that stuff left over."

She handed me a cup of steaming coffee. "Thought it might make you feel more welcome." She paled a little. "Can be intimidating landing in a new country for the first time."

Ah ... so that's how it was.

"Sure can." I sat at the four-seater table tucked into a corner of what was more like a kitchenette than a kitchen. "Will this be your first trip to the States?"

She grimaced. "My first trip overseas period." She leaned forward, her eyes wide. "I'm freaking terrified."

"You'll be fine." Girls like Annabelle always were. People were drawn to friendliness and all she'd need to do was bat her big blue eyes and use that broad accent and she'd have guys fawning all over her in Denver.

"Easy for you to say," she said, staring into her coffee mug. "You're confident and gorgeous." She lifted her gaze slowly to meet mine. "What if everyone over there takes one look at me and thinks I'm some hick Aussie who hasn't got a clue?"

Feeling strangely protective, I shook my head. "That won't happen. Besides, my BFF is at DU. I'll make sure she looks out for you."

Note to self: email Mia ASAP and let her know to take the Aussie under her wing.

"And her boyfriend's from Sydney, he's at DU too, so you'll know two people, okay?"

Annabelle clapped her hands in excitement as I struggled not to wince. "That'd be great. Thanks Dani, you're the best."

As Annabelle continued to prattle on about everything from the campus cafeteria to the best bohemian shops in Brunswick Street to her favorite cheese stall at the nearby

Queen Victoria Market, I learned that everything was 'the best'.

A long sixty minutes later, she'd given me the grand tour of the flat—small lounge, bathroom, kitchen, and bedroom—and given me access to Clarice, her bicycle, for my duration here.

After a drawn out goodbye that included three hugs, she bundled her bags and herself into a cab and thankfully headed for her parents' house for her last night in Melbourne, after extricating promises I'd email regularly.

I didn't dare not to, in case she changed her mind about six months at DU and came back early.

Oddly enough, the flat felt empty without Annabelle's incessant chatter and I wandered around aimlessly, eyelids heavy, craving sleep but knowing I needed to stay awake to beat the jetlag.

A quick glance in the fridge showed me Annabelle's priorities were screwed. She valued bedroom decoration above stocking food. One tub of strawberry yoghurt, half a bunch of celery and a bottled water wouldn't do much for the hunger gnawing a hole in my gut. Which meant I needed to find the nearest grocer or takeout ASAP ... on a bike.

Feeling like I'd regressed to my crappy childhood, I wheeled the bicycle—pink-trimmed, what else—down the hallway and out onto the tiny patio, remembering to pocket the key before I locked myself out.

A tram rumbled past as I stared at the bicycle. I hadn't ridden one since I was eight but hey, how hard could it be?

"Be nice, Clarice," I said, wondering who was crazier. Annabelle for naming her bike or me for talking to it.

I swung my leg over and settled onto the seat. Tried

coasting a little, balancing on the ground with my toes. Not so bad.

From the hand-drawn map on the fridge, I knew there was an all-night grocer two blocks away. I could easily fit staples like milk, cheese, bread and Oreos—hell, I hope they stocked Oreos in Australia—in the bike's basket.

Growing in confidence, I coasted a little faster, enjoying the balmy evening breeze in my hair. Time to try pedaling.

I'd managed one revolution. Another. Before I rounded a corner and slammed into something.

Or someone.

"What the fuck—" Strong arms reached out to steady me but it was too late.

We went down in a sprawling heap of metal and arms and legs, my cry of shock mingling with more vociferous swearing from the guy I'd just run over.

I hadn't seen him until the moment he sat up, the streetlight from above casting a halo over him.

But this guy was no angel. With the whole dark hair, dark eyes, permanent glower thing he had going on, he looked more like the devil as he glared at me.

"You bloody idiot. Don't you know the road rules?" He winced as he rubbed his elbow. "You shouldn't be riding on the footpath."

"Sorry, I didn't know."

His eyes narrowed with suspicion. "You're not faking that American accent to get off easy, are you?"

I shook my head, rather taken with his deep voice, even if he was growling at me. "I'm Californian. Just arrived today."

"Figures." He struggled into a kneeling position and straightened his back. "Here's a tip for you, Yank. Stay off the bike 'til you know the road rules here, can ride, or both."

"I can ride," I said, squaring my shoulders and wishing I hadn't as a bolt of pain shot between my blades.

"Badly," he said, the corners of his mouth easing into something resembling a smile.

"It's not funny. Clarice may be damaged for life."

"Clarice?" His eyebrows shot up as he shook his head. "Crazy American chick."

"Clueless Aussie dumbass," I responded, pushing into a squat. "I'm renting a flat for six months while I'm studying here and Clarice's owner has a thing for naming her bicycle."

I had no idea why I blurted that out, because I didn't give a shit what he thought about me. I'd apologize and be on my way, my dignity as bent out of shape as Clarice.

"You need to lighten up." He stood and held out his hand to me.

"Enough with the tips." Annoyed by his surliness, I ignored his hand and stood by myself. "If you're okay, I'm out of here—"

"Aussies are laid back. Relaxed. So if you want to fit in here, you need to lighten up."

He was a about a head taller than me and I hated that I had to tilt my head back to look him in the eye. "Nothing personal, but you'll get on with people a lot easier if you lose the uptight attitude."

God, he was supercilious and pretentious and seriously hot.

I'd been trying to ignore that last part but now that we stood almost toe-to-toe, I couldn't deny it. He was lean yet emanated a quiet strength. Chiseled cheekbones. Strong jaw. Incredibly dark eyes that challenged and taunted and held untold secrets.

And that's what captured my interest the most. The

secrets. I knew all about those. Knew how they dogged every night and every waking moment too.

It's the only reason that could explain my impulsive invitation as I said, "Do you want to have coffee? My shout. It's the least I can do after running you over. And being a complete Neanderthal when it comes to Aussie road rules."

I blabbered like an idiot, wishing he'd stop staring at me with those mesmerizing eyes and say something.

When the silence stretched toward uncomfortable, I knew I had to rescue Clarice and my pride and make a run for it. "Forget it—"

"Sure," he said, his tone noncommittal. "Though maybe we should put Clarice to bed and walk?"

To my utter shock, I felt heat surging to my cheeks. I never blushed. Ever. I'd done too much and seen too much to be embarrassed by anything. But hearing this guy discussing putting anything to bed made me hot all over.

"Okay." It wasn't until he'd picked up the mangled bike and fell into step beside me did I realize I'd violated my golden rule on my very first night in Melbourne.

Do not show the slightest interest in guys for the duration.

FOUR
ASHTON

My shit day had just got shittier.

Granted, I'd been mulling on the way back from visiting Mum, so probably hadn't been paying attention to where I was going, but being run over by a clumsy chick just topped off my crap day nicely.

Agreeing to have coffee with her? Bad move.

Last thing I needed was to make small talk with a stranger. Inevitable I'd inflict my foul mood on her, she'd crack the shits and I'd feel even worse than I did now.

Losing a mega commission this morning had set the tone for the day and it had gone downhill from there.

My paintings paid Mum's Special Accommodation fees. Without them? I couldn't comprehend what would happen if I had to take her out of the place she'd got accustomed to and relocate her in some grungy facility.

I'd toured several of those when it first became apparent she couldn't stay at home any more. They were dank, dismal, dreary dives filled with old people that smelled like death. Mum may have dementia but I couldn't allow her to waste away in a dump like that.

So I'd found Cool Waters, a private special accommodation nursing home that charged a small fortune but was worth every cent. The place had the feel of a boutique hotel rather than a lock up for people who'd lost their mind. And from that moment, I'd done everything in my power to ensure Mum never had to leave.

I'd shelved my dream of launching an art career in a major gallery. Instead, I'd sold the pieces I'd painstakingly stored over the last two years and I now worked for hire. Whoring my paintings. Taking on crummy commission work for families with too much money and not enough class. Doing whatever it took to pay the bills.

My tutoring job at Melbourne Uni? Barely enough to pay my rent and grab the occasional pizza. But I'd be damned if I whined or felt bad when Mum's life was effectively over.

"Where are we going?" American Chick strode alongside me, her long legs eating up the pavement.

"Lygon Street. Melbourne's Little Italy." Great, now I sounded like a frigging tourist guide. "Considering you're about to ply me with coffee to soothe my bruised bones, maybe I should know your name?"

"Dani." She laughed, the sweetest sound I'd heard in a long while, and damned if I didn't want to hear it again. "And you are?"

"Ashton." I felt like I should add 'but my friends call me Ash'. But I didn't have many of those any longer. My high school buddies thought I was a fag for being more interested in art than football. And my uni mates weren't too keen on hanging out with a guy who didn't have a spare cent to spend on partying.

I didn't mind being a loner. But it was times like this,

when I was in the company of a gorgeous girl, that I felt more out of my depth than ever.

"So what do you do, Ash, when you're not being run over by jetlagged women?"

I liked her teasing tone; liked that she'd lost the hard-edged glare; liked that she'd called me Ash as if it was the most natural thing in the world.

"I'm an artist," I said, curious to gauge her reaction as I shot her a sideways glance.

"That's great." She stopped, her eyes wide with enthusiasm. "I'm starting an art major."

She wrinkled her nose. "A twenty-one year old student who hopes the teens don't think I'm a weirdo art geek."

Increasingly enchanted by her, and annoyed because of it, I feigned indifference. "And are you?"

"A weirdo art geek?" She nodded, her grin proud. "Abso-frikking-lutely. Love everything to do with art."

Uh-oh. She just scored another ten Brownie points without trying.

She tilted her head to one side, studying me. "Do you teach art too?"

She obviously knew art, savvy enough to understand not many artists made enough to live off and had to supplement their income, usually by teaching.

"Do I look that old?"

"You look hot," she muttered, much to my delight, before rushing on, "I mean, you look mature and I'm a hopeless judge of age and most artists work too so I thought ... ah, fuck."

She chuckled and held up her hands. "I'm seriously jetlagged and making an absolute fool of myself. Think I'll just shut the hell up now."

At that moment, I found myself doing something I hadn't done in a long time.

I laughed.

"I think you should've quit when you said I was hot."

She winced, a faint pink staining her cheeks. "Can we forget I ever said that? Seriously. I barely slept on the plane and then I ran you over and I'm hungry—"

"Excuses will get you everywhere," I said, ducking down to murmur in her ear. "And if it makes you feel any better? The feeling's mutual."

I had no idea why I said that, other than the fact I hadn't flirted in forever. I couldn't remember the last time I'd had a date let alone got laid. I steered clear of the students with crushes or the ones who'd do anything—including sleep with me—to get better grades. And considering I couldn't afford to go out and party hard, I didn't meet a lot of women on the social scene.

God, I sounded like a sad case. I really needed to get a life, outside of the one I had as primary carer for Mum.

"So you're hungry too?" she said, her deliberate misinterpretation tempered with a wink. "Because if you think I'm hot, I may think the worst of you and assume when you agreed to have coffee with me, you thought you were getting *coffee*."

I admit it. I was a sucker for a woman with a sense of humor. Not only was Dani a hottie—sassy, tall blondes were definitely my type—she liked art and could have a laugh.

The fact I hadn't had sex in a long while? Was suddenly all I could think about and my cock agreed.

"Considering you almost broke my leg, you definitely owe me coffee."

Her smile made me feel like howling at the moon. A

primitive reaction unable to be contained, similar to my sudden yearning to know this woman on every level.

"Next you'll be asking me to rub it better." She rolled her eyes. "I'm jetlagged but not completely devoid of common sense."

Enjoying our sparring immensely, I continued, "Does that mean you'll be up for some rubbing once the jetlag wears off?"

"Down, big fella." She elbowed me. "Let's have coffee." She held up a finger and waggled it at me. "Just for the record? I'm in Melbourne for six months to study. And I've sworn off boys in the interim."

"Good to know." I paused, pretending to think, before giving in to impulse and reaching out to touch her arm. "Lucky for you, I'm all man."

FIVE
DANI

I was in *so* much trouble.

How pathetic was I that I couldn't stick to my 'no guys' mantra on my first night in Melbourne?

Then again, Ashton wasn't just any guy.

Sitting at an outdoor table at a charming roadside cafe, sipping a perfect latte and staring into his eyes, felt ... right.

Like I'd known him for a hundred years. Like he could *see* me and didn't find me lacking. Like I was good enough to be with someone like him.

"You look tired," he said, pushing a plate of biscotti toward me.

"If that's your version of sweet-talk, you need to work on your technique." I took my third piece and bit into the crisp, almond goodness. I was starving and once Ashton finished his obligatory coffee and left, I'd be ordering the biggest damn pizza I could find on the extensive menu.

The corners of his eyes crinkled adorably when he smiled. "You're the one who should be sweet-talking me."

"I've already apologized for running you over." I pointed

at his coffee mug. "And this is my treat. What more do you want?"

"You really want to know?" His eyes darkened to ebony as his gaze dropped to my mouth, and I could've sworn I flushed from my toes to the top of my head.

"Uh-huh." I managed to sound flippant as I reached for another biscotti and snapped it in two.

Way too casual and calm, he dunked his biscotti into his espresso before answering. "I want to know what kind of an exciting life you've led to defer your tertiary studies 'til now."

I never talked about myself, with anyone. Back home, I'd spent my life honing nonchalance into an art form. No one got close. Ever. But Ashton sounded wistful more than curious and I found myself leaning toward honesty.

"The truth? I'm a rich bitch with parents who are Hollywood sycophants. We've got the Beverly Hills mansion and the lifestyle to match. LA at its best." I hadn't realized I'd crumbled the biscotti in my hand to dust until I glanced down so I wouldn't meet his judgmental gaze. "I dropped out of college before I started. Partied hard instead. 'Til a recent epiphany and here I am."

I threw my arms wide, hating how shallow I sounded, hating how brittle I felt.

"Interesting," he said, his tone surprisingly devoid of derision or pity. "Though I was after more of an exposé than the cookie-cutter version."

I stiffened, startled by his perception. He'd immediately seen beneath my purposefully harsh portrayal of my life and wanted to know more.

As if.

Forcing a smile, I raised my cup in his direction. "For

that, you'd have to agree to dinner, and I can see you have places to be and people to see."

"Actually, I don't." He rested his forearms on the table, strong, lean forearms dusted with a light smattering of hair. "I can't think of the last time a beautiful woman asked me out to dinner, so if you're offering, sweetheart, I'm all yours."

My heart did a weird jive as he added with a smile, "For the next few hours, that is."

I should go. Cite tiredness and just scram. Not only was I hungry but something about this guy lowered my well-honed defenses in a way that terrified.

But my stomach rumbled at that moment, he heard and I found myself picking up a menu to scan the dinner specials.

"Sounds like I'm not the only one with a story to tell," I said, quickly settling on the fettuccini marinara in the hope a decent shot of carbs would calm my tumbling tummy. It had to be lack of food and not a sudden hunger for the intense guy sitting opposite. "How could someone like you not have a date every night of the week?"

He raised an eyebrow as he glanced at me over the top of the menu. "Someone like me?"

"Come on, you're too smart to fish for compliments." I rolled my eyes when he smirked. "Fine. You're articulate, smart and cute. So the fact you haven't had dinner with a woman in a while? Must have a story behind it."

"You forgot hot," he said, beckoning a waiter. "Women tend to go for hot apparently."

"You're insufferable," I said, unable to stop grinning as we stared at each other, invisible sparks arcing across the table, and making me wish I'd bolted while I still had the chance.

"And starving." He gestured at me when the waiter arrived. "What are you having?"

"Fettuccini marinara, please." With a side serve of Ashton. A huge helping all to myself, to taste and savor ... yum.

"And the linguini matriciana for me," he said, waiting until we were alone again before adding, "dinner's on me, by the way."

I shook my head. "Uh-uh. We'd already agreed. I ran you over, dinner's on me and Clarice."

He looked set to argue, so I added, "Besides, you'll shatter my illusion of a tortured, starving artist if you insist on paying."

He stiffened, and his lips compressed, as I silently cursed my big mouth. Looks like I'd hit a nerve.

Just when I thought I'd have to cover my gaff with some lame-ass joke, he relaxed into his chair a little.

"You're not far off the mark," he said, draining his water glass before linking his hands and stretching, an action that pulled his T shirt up, revealing a sliver of taut, tanned skin that had me salivating more than the delicious aromas wafting out of the restaurant kitchen. "Sorry to say, but I'm an artist cliché."

Surprised he was man enough to admit to hardship—most guys would rather bullshit than show weakness—I gave him time to continue.

"I'm a tutor at the uni, and I sell paintings by commission on the side." His mocking tone made it sound like he sold his body rather than art. "Not exactly Beverly Hills standard."

I snorted. "'Course not, because you're actually making a real living, not existing in some fake fantasy world."

I picked at a piece of fresh bread, peeling back the

crispy crust, shocked by the uncharacteristic urge to unburden myself to a virtual stranger. "Where I come from? The world in which I grew up? Is so far from reality it'd make your head spin."

I'd shredded the bread before I knew I'd done it and I had to sit on my hands to stop from fiddling. "Sometimes it's good to escape reality, but there eventually comes a point where you realize there's more to life than all that shit."

"And that's when you board a plane for Australia, right?"

He had no idea how accurate that was.

"Yep. The escape artist, that's me." I smiled, when inside I felt sick at how close I'd come to saying so much more.

"Nice pun." He studied me, his stare too intense, too perceptive, too much. "So what are you really running from?"

Everything. But I wisely kept that gem to myself.

"I prefer to see it as what I'm running toward." I picked up my wine glass and raised it at him. "Here's to a new city, a new start and a new friend."

To my relief, he picked up his glass and clinked it against mine. "Maybe if you take Clarice out for another spin tomorrow, you can run over a few more people and make even more friends."

I smiled. "Why? When the first guy I've run over is so damn special?"

When he smiled back at me, I could've sworn the entire street lit up in fireworks.

"Welcome to Melbourne, Dani." This time when he clinked my glass, his gaze locked on mine and I couldn't look away. I didn't want to.

Damn, I was in so much trouble.

SIX
ASHTON

This wasn't me.

One minute I'd been walking home from visiting Mum, the next I was sitting at an outdoor cafe in Lygon Street, talking and flirting and having dinner with a virtual stranger.

I should've said no when Dani invited me for a coffee. And I should've definitely said no when she suggested we have dinner. But I hadn't been able to refuse for one simple fact.

She seemed lost.

Not in the geographical sense, but on an intrinsic level that brought out every protective instinct I had.

There was something in her eyes ... a bleakness, a loneliness, a lack of hope, that called to me, because I knew exactly how she felt.

Seeing Mum like that today? Really threw me. And made me so damn mad I could punch something. So I'd been stewing instead, railing against the injustices of the world, when Dani had run me over. Fate's way of telling me to stop being a whiny pain in the arse? If so, fate had damn fine taste, because Dani was seriously sexy.

"I've come to a very important decision," she said, sitting back and patting her stomach. "While I'm here, I'm going to visit every restaurant and cafe along this street and sample their best dish."

Trying not to stare at her flat stomach—and failing—I said, "Then I'm guessing you'll be taking Clarice for a long ride every day to counteract the carbs?"

I'd meant it as a joke. A pretty dumb one when her smile faded. "You sound like my Mom."

"Sorry."

She waved away my apology. "Not your fault. Touchy subject."

Was that behind Dani's inherent sadness? An eating disorder?

"My Mom paid a bit of attention to me when I was younger, long enough to tell me what to wear, what to eat and what to play. When I didn't do as she said, she lost interest." She shrugged. "We lived in the same house but I rarely saw my folks."

"That's tough." But not as tough as watching my Mum drink herself into dementia.

"What about your folks? What are they like?"

Damn. This is what came of being too buddy-buddy with someone. I wanted to lie, to make up some story to fob her off, but when Dani stared at me with those big, soulful eyes, I found myself unable to formulate a half-truth.

"Mum was an actress. Never knew my father. Some producer she dated for a short time who left for New York and she never bothered to contact again."

"Was?" Sadness pinched her mouth. "I'm so sorry, Ash, I didn't realize she was dead."

"She's not, just retired." And that was all I was willing to give. "I've got a ton of marking to do tonight. I'll walk you back?"

"Okay." Her way-too-astute stare lost some of its solemnness. "We can leave now."

"But the bill—"

"Already taken care of when I ducked inside to ask for more water." She stood. "And before that male pride of yours takes a beating and you get all high and mighty with me, just forget it, okay?" She grinned. "Next one's on you."

"There's going to be a next time?" Damned if my heart didn't leap in anticipation at the thought.

"Seeing as you're my only friend in this place, absolutely." When I stood, she slipped her hand into mine, like it was the most natural thing in the world. "And when I say friend, I mean friend."

She hesitated, gnawing on her lower lip, a perfectly normal action that shot straight to my groin. "I'm done with dating for a while. So while I'm in Melbourne, I'm going to concentrate on my studies." She swung our arms back and forth. "Friends is good."

Friends was bad. Because what I felt for Dani? Was distinctly unfriendly.

I wanted to take her back to my place and shag her until dawn. Hot, sweaty, raunchy sex. Complication-free. A simple physical connection to take the edge off this buzz I'd been feeling since we met.

"Who said anything about dating?" I shot her a sideways glance as we fell into step. "Bonking buddies would suit me just fine."

I expected her to laugh. I didn't expect her to stop dead, release my hand and turn to face me, uncertainty clouding her eyes. "Is that the same as a fuck buddy? Friends with benefits?"

"Yeah," I said, not sure where this was going and wishing I'd kept my big mouth shut.

"Hmm ..." She deliberately looked me up and down, and I swear it felt like she'd touched me everywhere she looked. "Let me think about it."

"I meant it as a joke." A half-hearted joke tinged with truth.

"Too bad." The corners of her mouth curved into a seductive smile that made me want to kiss her senseless. "Because I have a weakness for hot, Aussie artists."

Before I could respond, she practically skipped ahead, flinging over her shoulder, "Coming?"

I sure as hell hoped so as I followed, lengthening my strides to catch up with her, increasingly aware I'd do everything in my power to turn my throwaway bonking buddies comment into reality.

SEVEN
DANI

Hell no. *No, no, no, no, no.*

I was *not* going to drag Ashton inside and have my wicked way with him, no matter how much I wanted to.

And I wanted. Big time. My body craved him like I'd once craved my next tequila shot. I tingled with it. All over.

He'd almost succeeded in making me hate him with that casual fuck buddy comment. Until I realized something. A guy who hadn't had dinner with a woman in ages wasn't the casual sex type. Which meant one of two things: it genuinely was a joke or Ashton wasn't interested in being friends with me.

Considering he'd stuck around and had dinner, it probably wasn't the latter. We'd talked. A lot. Mostly about college life here in Australia. And art.

The guy knew his stuff and I found myself hanging on his every word as he enlightened me on the best local galleries to iconic Aussie artists.

When he'd offered some of his books, had told me to come by his office at the university any time, I'd almost jumped on the table and danced a jig of joy.

Because for the first time ever, I'd met a guy who was deeper than a shallow puddle.

And that offer of dropping by his office on the pretext of borrowing books? Meant he did want to see me again, no matter how cool he'd played it over dinner.

We were almost back to the apartment and stupidly I wanted to prolong this evening as long as possible.

"So what do you do for fun in this city?"

He snorted. "I'm the last person to give advice on the latest hot spots."

"Don't go out much?"

"Try never," he muttered, sounding bitter. "Not much time between tutoring all day and painting all night."

"And you're having a ball doing it, if your unbridled enthusiasm is any indication."

We stopped outside my apartment and he managed a small smile. "Bet you think I'm a weirdo recluse."

He didn't want to know what I thought. Because if I articulated half of what I was thinking right now? He'd run because he'd think I was the weirdo.

I shrugged. "It's not so bad being a hermit."

"Coming from a self-confessed party girl, I think you just insulted me." His lips quirked into an adorable smile. "Trust me, our social lives are worlds apart."

"Maybe I can convince you to shake things up a little?" Not that I was particularly interested in doing the club circuit in Melbourne. Far from it. But if I played up the clueless tourist angle, Ashton would take pity on me and insist on showing me around.

I could live in hope, right?

"I don't do the social scene." He thrust his hands into his pockets, rocking on the balls of his feet like he couldn't wait to escape. "Thanks for dinner."

"Pleasure."

We stood there, a foot apart, awkward and silent and strangely shy.

If this were the old me back in LA, I'd be all over the guy already. Dragging him inside for a bout of quickie sex, doing whatever it took to stave off the soul-destroying memories that overcame me when I was alone.

Loneliness was not my friend. But I wanted Ashton to be, and that meant saying goodbye before I did something stupid, like resurrect my old ways no matter how much I wanted to put them behind me.

I took a tentative step toward him, before thinking better of it. "Just so you know? I like you. And because I like you, I'm not going to do anything more than this."

Before I could second guess myself, I placed a quick kiss on his cheek. Then I backed away before the warmth of his skin and his subtle masculine scent made me do what I really wanted to do: climb all over him.

"Dani ..."

I didn't wait to hear the rest of what he had to say. Because if I stuck around any longer I wouldn't want him to leave.

"I'll see you round." With that, I turned and ran, bounding up the steps to the apartment, fumbling with the keys and eventually making it inside.

It wasn't until I slammed the door shut and leaned against it that I exhaled in relief.

I'd done it.

Managed to stave off the need to obliterate the memories.

I should feel good.

So why did I feel so goddamn bad?

EIGHT
ASHTON

When I re-read the same paragraph for the fifth time, I pushed away from my desk. I had a stack of essays on Monet to mark and had managed to do three of them before the usual morning rush of students had traipsed through my office.

But that wasn't the real reason for my distraction.

That honor lay with Dani.

It had been four days since I'd met her, ninety-six hours since our dinner, and I couldn't stop thinking about her.

She invaded my thoughts constantly; whether I was listening to self-absorbed students try to sway me with pathetic excuses why their assignments were late or while painting into the wee small hours, I replayed our dinner in detail.

The way she'd absentmindedly twirled her hair around her finger when she was listening, the way she ate like it was her last meal, the way she looked at me when she thought I couldn't see: like I was dessert and she wanted to gobble me in one go.

Which was odd, considering her adamant stance to just

be friends. We'd flirted a little, we'd skirted a lot. Skirted around the attraction sizzling between us. Fine by me, because the last thing I needed in my life right now was a girlfriend. Between work and commissions and Mum, I didn't have time for anything else.

But for a few hours last Friday evening, I'd actually forgotten the constant pressures weighing me down, and allowed myself to have fun.

It had been liberating and I'd ended up painting all weekend. Not commissions, but a series of abstracts I'd been working on in my very limited spare time.

Having Dani as my muse might've been inspiring during my downtime, but when I'd entered my office here on Monday morning? Remembering her—how she'd smiled, how she'd held my hand, how she'd kissed me on the cheek - had been a serious distraction.

I linked my hands and stretched overhead, working out the kinks in my back. As I bent backward, I spied the row of hardbacks on the top shelf. The books I'd offered to Dani.

I'd been pleased to hear she preferred paperbacks and hardbacks books to research her art rather than the Internet. I was the same, hence my extensive collection.

The part where I'd invited her to borrow whatever she liked? Had surprised the hell out of me.

If I had no time for dating, I definitely had no time for a friend. But the fact I jumped whenever a knock sounded at my door pretty much told me what I already knew: that I was looking forward to seeing Dani again, despite all self-talk to the contrary.

My gaze fell on my laptop next to the stack of papers on my desk and I remembered the countless online assignments I also had to mark. Throw in the five student appointments this afternoon and a deadline on a commission brought forward by three days by a demanding snobby diva, and I didn't have time to breathe.

Which didn't stop me practically bolting to the door when I heard a faint knock.

I opened it to find Dani clutching a giant bag filled with notebooks and a laptop, her tentative smile hitting me where I feared it most: my heart.

"Your offer to loan me those books still stand?"

I nodded and stepped back from the open door. "Yeah, but I'm really swamped."

"I won't stay long." Her smile faded and I mentally kicked myself. "Though I can probably only carry a few or Clarice will complain."

"That's one temperamental bike." I rubbed my thigh and fake winced. "I hope her dents aren't as bad as mine."

"She's fine." Her gaze pinned me with questions I had no hope of answering. Questions like 'why the cold reception when we connected last week? Why offer me the books if you didn't want to see me again? Why are you being such a jerk?'

Hating how uncertain I felt around her, I pointed to the top shelf. "The books are up there. If you need any recommendations, give a yell."

With that, I completed my arse-hole act by turning my back on her, taking a seat at my desk and pretending to read the assignment I'd already tried to read several times.

I heard a stifled snort behind me and resisted the urge to leap off my chair, bundle her into my arms and kiss her senseless.

Fuck, this was crazy. My body was fairly vibrating with tension, I couldn't concentrate on anything and I had a hard-on that wouldn't quit.

When Dani laid a hand on my shoulder, I swear I jumped a foot.

"What?" I snapped, instantly regretting my abrupt response when I caught sight of her expression: a cross between a deer caught in headlights and a wounded puppy.

"I've got a problem."

"If you need help getting them down—"

"My problem is you." She towered over me, arms folded, so I stood, not realizing until it was too late that we were almost toe-to-toe. "I thought you were serious about us being friends but obviously I was wrong. You're a jackass."

She poked me in the chest. "And you can take your arty-farty books and shove them up your ass."

I deserved her derision, and worse. But when I saw a shimmer in her eyes that looked suspiciously like tears, I couldn't take it anymore.

I grabbed her arm. "Don't go."

She stared at my hand like it was dog-shit she'd stepped in. "Let go of me."

So I did. But then I did something even dumber.

I kissed her.

A no-holds-barred slamming of my mouth against hers, the connection of our lips as sizzling as I'd fantasized.

I expected her to push me away.

I didn't expect for her to combust.

She went wild. There was no other word for it as she pushed me against the desk so hard my butt dislodged the assignments and they tumbled to the floor.

I didn't care. I didn't care about anything bar getting more of *this*. This incredibly, mind-blowing sensation of hot, open-mouthed kisses that went on forever. The kind of kisses to make me forget all the bad stuff. The kind of kisses that almost made me believe all was right with the world.

Her hands fisted my T-shirt. My hands grabbed her arse.

When she writhed against me, pure perfection.

I throbbed with wanting her. All of her. Me deep inside, her clenching around me.

She pulled away, staring at me with those big blue eyes that made me want to do it all over again.

"You're an idiot," she said, her breathing as ragged as mine.

"Tell me something I don't know." I rubbed the back of my neck. Did little for the tension there. "Sorry."

She snorted. "You can stick that apology the same place as your books."

A bark of laughter erupted from me. "Guess I deserved that."

"You did." She folded her arms and I struggled not to stare at her chest. "When I hurt you, I bought you dinner." The corners of her adorable mouth twitched. "So now you've hurt me, guess you owe me lunch."

I didn't want to spend time with Dani. Especially after that kiss. If I hadn't been able to get her out of my mind before, I didn't have a hope in hell now. The less time I spent with her, the better.

But by the determined glint in her eyes, she wasn't going to let me off the hook.

"Can't I just loan you the books and call it quits?"

She shook her head. "I'll see you for lunch at that park near my place today." Her gaze drifted to the top shelf. "I'll borrow the impressionists text and save the rest for when I want to come by to bug you some more."

I shrugged. "Whatever," I said, sounding like a six-year-old.

She grinned, pulled the mini step ladder I had in the

corner over to the bookshelf, and climbed up to reach for the book. I'd never been so glad to see her wearing jeans, because if she had a skirt on? She wouldn't be leaving this office for the next hour. Maybe two.

"What do you want for lunch?"

"Surprise me." She glanced over her shoulder, a beguiling mix of mischievous and playful. "As long as it hasn't got anchovies in it."

"One garlic pizza with an extra serve of anchovies coming up." I liked teasing her, liked seeing the green flecks highlighted in her eyes when she was feisty.

She snorted and climbed down the ladder. "You better give me your cell number too."

"You mean my mobile phone number?"

She rolled her eyes. "Yeah, Aussie boy."

"Seeing as you asked so nicely." I held out my hand. "Give me your *cell* and I'll program it in."

I didn't want to give Dani my number but it would make things easier in the long run. Like if I didn't want to see her, texting would be better than face-to-face let-downs.

Her eyes narrowed. "Knowing you, you'd deliberately program a wrong number, so why don't you just tell me?"

I laughed. How did she know me so well in such a short space of time? "I could tell you a wrong number too."

"You won't." She brandished my textbook. "A geek who keeps hardbacks like this values his books and as long as I have it, you'll behave."

"You're holding my book to ransom?"

"Yep." She nodded and a strand of long blonde hair clung to her cheek. I itched to brush it away, to twist it around my finger, to bring her within kissing distance again ...

"Just go." I rattled off my mobile number, the real one, needing her gone before I followed through on my thoughts.

"See you at the park at one." She stuffed my book into her overflowing bag and headed for the door. She paused, her hand on the doorknob. "What was that kiss about?"

Damn, I thought I'd gotten away with not talking about it.

I shrugged. "You're very kissable."

Her lips curved into a smile that took my breath away. "I know we're just friends but for the record?" She fanned herself. "It was frikking hot."

"Yeah," was all I could mumble as our gazes locked, the electricity arcing between us.

I could've sworn there was a ringing in my ears as neither of us moved, remembering that kiss, yearning to do it again.

If she made a move toward me, I'd be locking the door and taking her up against it.

After what seemed like an eternity, she blinked, turned her back and walked out.

I should've been relieved.

I wasn't.

I wanted her more than ever.

NINE
DANI

I wasn't a patient person at the best of times so when Ashton was fifteen minutes late for lunch I pulled out my cell to check for messages. To belatedly realize he'd given me his number but hadn't asked for mine.

"Damn," I muttered, flipping the cell over and over in my hand.

Fifteen minutes wasn't all that late. He could've run overtime with a tutoring session or got caught up in marking and forgot the time. But as I scanned the park, I had a sinking feeling there was more behind Ashton's tardiness than work.

I'd been so freaked out by our kiss I'd skipped my next class—something I couldn't afford to do—and hunkered down in the library instead. I'd found the quietest corral in the furthest corner, flipped open his book and pretended to read, replaying that kiss in my mind the entire time.

When I'd told him it was hot? Big understatement. Huge. Because when Ash kissed me? I'd felt ... almost whole. Like it was right. Like I could never do anything dumb again as long as I was in his arms and he was kissing me.

It had been a long while since I'd felt like that, if ever. And I wanted to feel it again. Which meant my stance on not getting involved with boys while I was in Melbourne? Under serious review.

Ashton wasn't like the losers I'd hung out with in LA. He was earnest and focused and unflappable. Who knew, maybe someone like him would be good for me. He could be part of my new start on the straight and narrow.

Yeah, and I could justify anything when it came to moving beyond friendship with a guy who kissed like a dream.

I waited another fifteen minutes before caving and texting him. I hated those needy chicks that constantly had to know where their men were and what they were doing but that bad feeling in my gut had intensified.

If Ash had freaked half as much as I had after that kiss, was he standing me up?

His reply came ten seconds later.

SORRY. CAN'T MAKE IT.

That was it. No suggestion of a rain check. No sign off. Nada.

Helplessness rolled over me, the same kind of helplessness that made me do stupid things back in LA, like getting so drunk I couldn't remember what I was doing or who I was doing it with.

I liked this guy. Really liked him.

The way we'd talked over dinner, the way we sparked off each other, suggested he could make my life in Melbourne over the next six months a hell of a lot easier.

I wasn't interested in making a heap of friends while I was here, despite the invitations I'd already had this week.

For some unfathomable reason, I gave off a vibe to the party crowd and they'd plied me with invites for anything from pub-crawls to housewarmings.

I got it; I was the new chick, an American, and that made me cooler somehow. But if I accepted those invitations and started partying in my first week here, I knew I wouldn't have the willpower to stop and I'd end up spiraling out of control into a lifestyle I'd vowed to escape.

So I'd stayed in every night. Pretending to study, thinking of Ash. His influence would be good for me. Stability when I was tempted to go a little crazy again.

So I didn't fire off an angry message, something along the lines of FUCK U.

Instead, I took the mature approach.

OK. C U SOON.

Short. Sweet. In the same casual tone as his.

Let him mull that kiss for a while longer. Let him stew.

Then I'd issue an invitation he couldn't refuse.

TEN
ASHTON

I shouldn't have caved.

Hanging out at Dani's flat on a Friday night was a disaster just waiting to happen.

But after standing her up for lunch, I'd felt bad and agreed to meet when she'd sent me a text asking for help with her first assignment.

Just because I'd freaked over that kiss didn't mean I had to act like a prick and take it out on her. I was a tutor. If she were any other student asking for help, I wouldn't hesitate.

So that's why I'd come. Why I'd agreed to share a pizza while we worked. Why I was still here, working on the last essay question while she stared at me with something other than study on her mind.

"Want a beer?"

"No thanks, I'm right," I said, trying to ignore the way her cotton yoga pants clung to her butt as she bent forward to grab a drink from the fridge.

Thankfully, I'd averted my gaze by the time she straightened and toasted me with a can of soft drink.

"I used to do vodkas, follow them up with tequila shots,

finish with a few beer chasers," she said, padding toward me, her bare feet barely making a sound on the pocked floorboards. "Now I'm such a goody-goody, I stick to this."

She raised her can in my direction again as she sat beside me, way too close for comfort. I could smell the fruity soap she used, could feel the heat radiating off her.

When she put the soft drink down on the table, she turned to me, studying me with a slightly quizzical expression. "What about you, Ash? Have you always been a goody-goody?"

She touched my arm, the barest brush of her fingertips against my skin, and I felt like I'd been electrocuted. "Or have you also been bad?"

I gritted my teeth against the urge to shove her assignment off the table and spread her across it.

"Who says I'm a goody-goody?" I finally managed when she stopped touching me.

She looked me up and down with a defiance that begged me to differ. "I've hung around with enough losers to know you're one of the good guys."

Faint praise. "Boyfriends?"

Not that I should care, but I did. I didn't like hearing the hint of sadness in her voice, like she'd seen too much, done too much.

"If you want to call them that," she said, her sorrow underscored with a brittle edge. "Casual. No-one serious."

She clasped her hands so tightly together I saw her knuckles whiten. It made me wonder which dickhead had done a number on her. And how I could find him to punch his lights out.

"I screwed up when I finished high school. Didn't go to college. Then spent the next three years trying to forget how I screwed up by hanging out with dipshits worse than me." Her tone cracked a little at the end and I couldn't resist sneaking an arm out to slide around her waist.

A normal instinct to comfort, nothing more. Then why the insane urge to hold her close all night long?

"You're here now," I said, sounding way too trite.

"I guess so." She tilted her head back to look at me and what I saw in her eyes made me blink.

Loss. Heart-wrenching loss that had left her bereft.

"What happened to you?" I murmured, capturing her chin in one hand while the other around her waist tugged her closer.

I didn't expect her to respond. Dani barely knew me and by the looks of her, she'd gone through some serious shit. Besides, why would she trust a guy who reneged on a friendship and blew colder than the Antarctic wind on a frigid Melbourne day?

"You don't want to know," she said, shaking her head so hard her ponytail whipped my cheek.

I didn't push her for answers. I didn't push her away. Instead, I hauled her into my arms and hugged her so tight my arms ached.

It should've ended there. A comforting hug. An apologetic hug from an arse-hole like me to a wounded girl like her.

But it didn't end there and I guess I'd known on some instinctual level that the next time we touched following that combustible kiss, we wouldn't be able to stop.

She snuggled into me, her nose snuffling my neck and damned if I didn't get a hard-on just by holding her.

I tried to disengage. She wouldn't let me. Her arms snaked around my middle as she wriggled onto my lap.

Fuck.

The feel of her butt against my cock? More than I could

stand and when she eased back to stare up at me with blatant need, I couldn't resist.

I kissed her with every ounce of pent-up frustration, an awkward clash of lips and tongue and teeth, like we were doing this for the first time and were clueless.

Logic insisted I push her away, walk out the door and avoid future contact. But the part of me buried deep that yearned for a connection, even a transient physical contact, knew I couldn't walk away from this girl no matter how much I tried.

I had no idea how long we kissed. A minute. An hour. Soul-destroying kisses that were so damned erotic I ached to be inside her.

But I didn't rush it. I wanted to savor every incredible moment of having Dani in my arms.

When we finally came up for air, she straddled me.

"I want you to spend the night," she said, cupping my face in her hands, ensuring I had nowhere to look but directly into her passion-hazed eyes.

"Like a slumber party, you mean?"

She smiled. "Did you bring PJs?"

"No."

Her palm rasped against my stubble. "Sleeping bag?"

"Uh-uh."

Her hand came to rest on my chest, directly over my heart that thundered like a wild thing. "Then I guess you'll be sleeping naked in my bed."

I screwed up my eyes, pretending to ponder. "Will there be a midnight feast?"

Her hand inched lower, her fingers toying with the button on my jeans. "You better believe it."

I couldn't wait any longer. The verbal foreplay with

Dani was as big a turn-on as having her ready, willing and able on my lap.

"In that case, we've got a good four hours to work up an appetite beforehand." I scooped her up like she weighed nothing, enjoying her girly squeals.

"Put me down, you big dufus." Though she didn't resist, considering her arms snaked around my neck and hung on. "But in case you're wondering, my bedroom's that first door down the hallway."

I didn't need to be told twice as I all but ran toward it. When I reached the door, I nudged it open with my hip and zeroed in on the one place I wanted to be right now. The bed.

But then Dani clapped her hands and a noise-activated lamp switched on, giving me more to look at than the shadowed outline of a bed.

"What the hell?" I laughed, gently depositing Dani on the bed before doing a three-sixty. "Are you running a souvenir shop from home?"

"The girl who rents this place, Annabelle, thought this stuff would make me feel welcome." She chuckled. "My favorite's the echidna jewelry holder."

"She went to a lot of trouble." I hadn't seen this much Australiana in one place since the university threw a party for the new students during orientation week when it coincided with Australia Day.

"Yeah, she did." A hint of sadness had returned to her tone. "Not many people would do stuff like this."

She didn't add 'for me' but I could hear it in her voice, could see it in the quick look away.

So I did the only thing I could to banish her sadness.

I reached for her.

She took my outstretched hands, let me tug her into standing.

"Will you let me do something for you tonight?" I asked, shocked by a surge of protectiveness so fierce that I'd fight all her battles if she let me. "Will you let me make you feel as incredible as you make me feel?"

The moment the words spilled from my lips, I wondered if it was too much. Would she freak out and think I was coming on too strong?

I had my answer when she nodded, grabbed the hem of my T-shirt, and peeled it upward.

I lifted my arms to help, waiting until she'd tossed it away before returning the favor. My fingertips deliberately grazed the soft skin of her waist. Higher. Across the undersides of her tits encased in black lace.

She whimpered, a purely needy sound that shot straight to my cock.

The rest happened faster than I would've liked, but considering the length of time since I'd last had sex, I needed to be inside her ASAP.

I knelt, ripped down her yoga pants, and her panties came with them. Leaving me eye level with her Brazilian. And nirvana.

I gripped her butt and tugged her toward me. Brushed my nose against her, inhaling the pungent musk of her arousal.

Then I licked her. Swiping my tongue over her clit repeatedly. Harder. Faster. Until her hands fisted in my hair and she cried out, her knees buckling slightly.

I eased her onto the bed and stood, making sure she was looking at me before I licked my lips.

"You're incredibly good at that," she murmured, her

cheeks flushed as she unhooked her bra and flung it away. "Now let me show you something I'm good at."

She scooted forward, unsnapped my jeans, tugged the zipper down and eased my jeans over my hips.

Her eyes widened when she caught sight of my cock. "You're going commando?"

"Haven't had time to do laundry this week."

What with the manic work hours to obliterate my constant thoughts of Dani and how much I'd wanted to do exactly what we were about to do.

"Impressive." I didn't know if she was talking about my daring or my cock, and I didn't care, when she pushed my jeans all the way down and I kicked them off.

When her hand wrapped around me, I was in heaven.

When her mouth closed around the tip of my cock, I groaned.

When she took me all the way into her mouth, I had to put a stop to this.

I didn't want my first time coming with her to be like this.

"Dani," I moaned, easing my hips back. "Later." Because the sight of her giving me a blowjob was something I'd never forget. "I need to be inside you so badly."

She glanced up at me from her kneeling position, the devilish glint in her eyes making her look like an angel hellbent on sin. "Okay, but I'm going to finish this later."

"Deal." As she stood, I grabbed a condom out of my wallet, wishing I were the kind of optimistic guy who packed three.

She stared at the foil packet. "You only have one?"

"Better make it count."

She plucked it from my fingers, tore it open and had me sheathed with an expertise that made me oddly jealous.

"Lucky for us, along with Aussie souvenirs, Annabelle stocks condoms in her bedroom."

She pointed at the single drawer bedside table. "So how about it? Ready to make good on that promise to make me feel incredible?"

"Absolutely."

And I did.

All night long.

ELEVEN
DANI

I woke to the shower running. Meant Ash hadn't bolted at daybreak like I'd expected.

Most women would take it as a good sign. Me? I wasn't so sure. I'd never done morning-after etiquette. Ever.

My sexual dalliances ended the moment mutual satisfaction was achieved. I never stayed the night. And I *never* let them spend the night.

Which meant having Ashton sleep over was a first on many levels. The first time I'd had sex four times in one night. The first time I'd come every time. The first time I'd let a guy spoon me until dawn.

Initially, it had been a game to me. See how long before I could make him crack. I'd been seriously pissed when he'd stood me up for lunch so had invited him here with one thing in mind.

Seduction.

But that plan had gone to shit the moment I'd started blabbing about my past ... what was it about this guy that had me wanting to confide?

Luckily, his comforting had ended up with the two of us

exactly where I'd wanted to be: in bed. I should be over him now. That's what usually happened when I had the slightest attraction to any guy back in LA. A bit of transient sex before moving on.

But looked like I was taking this new life start-over seriously, because the way I was feeling right now? Not over Ash. Far from it. Not even remotely.

I wanted more. More of him. More of what we'd shared last night. More of this insane, glorious feeling making me tingle from head to foot, a feeling I suspected bordered on happiness.

I'd never been truly happy. Not at any stage of my life. All those gifts my folks showered me with to appease their consciences? The guys I'd slept with? The vacations to ritzy resorts? I would've traded them all to feel one ounce of what I was feeling now.

My friendship with Mia was the closest thing I'd had to being happy, but even that had been underscored by my guilt at not telling her everything. It had tainted us. Culminating in the disastrous fuck-up that had led me here to get my life back on track.

Sleeping with Ash may not have been terribly smart considering my grand plan to stay away from guys and focus on my studies. But Ash wasn't just any guy. He was the only friend I had here and the connection we shared counted for something. Something beyond sex.

That thought alone propelled me out of bed and toward the bathroom. I needed to see that the sex hadn't changed us. That he could still look at me with that intoxicating mix of mischief and seriousness. My naughty geek, that's how I'd come to think of him. For someone so somber most of the time, he could do wicked things in the bedroom.

He glanced over his shoulder and spotted me through

the fogged shower screen the moment I stepped into the bathroom. I waited, holding my breath. Waited for him to turn off the taps so he could leave me to shower alone. Waited for him to ask me to give him another few minutes. Waited for him to shut down.

When his lips curved into the sexy smile I remembered from last night, my heart leapt. And when he opened the shower door and beckoned me with a crook of his finger, I didn't need to be asked twice.

"Good morning," he said, turning to envelop me in his arms, the evidence of exactly how good it was jutting into my belly.

"It is now." I slid my arms around his neck, backed him up a little, so the water cascaded over both of us.

"Thanks." He rested his forehead against mine, a strangely intimate gesture that got to me more than our slick bodies pressed together.

"For what?"

"For a night I'll never forget." His lips brushed mine in a slow, sensual sweep that made me sag against him. "For being warm and fun and spontaneous." He nibbled his way along my jaw toward my ear. "For being amazing in bed." He sucked my earlobe into his mouth and tongued it. "Most of all, for being you."

Thank God for the water spraying us because the last thing I needed was for him to see how his words had moved me to tears.

I kissed him, a desperate melding of mouths to obliterate the terror coursing through me.

I didn't cry over guys. I didn't feel more than lust. And I sure as hell didn't let a little sweet-talking get to me.

So I did the one thing guaranteed to distract us both.

I kissed my way down his chest. Across his hips. His upper thighs. Before taking him into my mouth.

I could do this. This I knew. A blowjob to take the edge off for him, to take the edge off my feelings. And I needed that more than anything, something familiar amidst this confusing, riotous, out of control feeling that was making me go a little nuts.

Ash could never be my forever guy.

But that didn't stop me wishing he could be.

～

I WASN'T the touristy type.

I'd come to Melbourne to do one thing: start over. Sure, I'd flicked through the guides Annabelle had left for me and thought a few things looked interesting, but I'd been too busy trying to get my head around lectures and assignments to worry about checking out Melbourne.

Oh, and there'd been that other distraction. The same distraction that was currently holding my hand as we strolled along Brunswick Street, one of the city's cultural hot spots.

Another thing that was new. I didn't do handholding. Guess I'd never liked any of my dates enough to let them touch me that long. With Ash, I kinda liked it.

I'd expected him to bolt after our steamy shower interlude this morning. Revert to reserved. Maybe even awkward. But having sex seemed to have eased some of his tension and he was almost comfortable around me.

Then he'd surprised me even more by suggesting he show me tourist haunts along his favorite street. I could've begged off on the pretext of doing Saturday grocery shopping or catching up on assignments or a study date in the library. Instead, I'd found myself trawling vintage shops, exploring cafes and gardening boutiques all day.

It had been the best twenty-four hours of my life.

Which made me want to run back to the apartment as fast as humanly possible.

I didn't deserve this kind of happiness. It made me feel guilty, that my baby had died because of what I'd done yet here I was, living it up.

Crazy, I know, because people suffered losses every day and moved on, but whenever I felt good, the guilt would be there, eating away at me, making me do dumb things.

Like sabotage the best relationship, the only relationship, I'd ever had.

Not that I was foolish enough to label what I had with Ash as a relationship. But we'd moved past friendship last night and I didn't know what to call us. Fuck buddies? Too crass, considering we knew stuff about each other beyond the physical.

Whatever we were, I was going to enjoy it for today. Time enough for my usual self-recriminations tomorrow.

"There's a great African restaurant a little further up. Want to have dinner?" He squeezed my hand, totally at ease with this new us.

"Sounds good." I squeezed back, wondering if he could see my happiness. "Though you're not sick of me yet? It's been a long day."

"It's been a great day," he said, tugging my hand so I landed flush against him. "Phenomenal."

"Agreed." I snuggled into him, feeling secure in a way I never had. "Though for a while there I was starting to doubt your masculinity, what with your never-ending supply of patience while I tried on dresses in every vintage shop along the street?"

The corners of his eyes crinkled as he smiled and pressed his pelvis into mine. "I thought last night would've allayed any doubts about my masculinity."

"Good point." I ran my fingers through his hair, savoring the silkiness. "Maybe you can prove it to me again after dinner?"

For me to want to spend another night with Ash? The equivalent of a full-blown declaration 'I seriously like you'. I was putting myself out there in a way I never had before.

He grimaced and my heart sank. "Sorry, I can't."

"Another hot date?" I aimed for levity, desperate to hide my hurt at his rejection.

He shook his head. "No, just promised I'd visit someone."

On a Saturday night?

God, I'd been an idiot. How could I have confused a mutual attraction and hot sex for anything more?

Of course Ash would have other girl friends. For all I knew, he could have an entire black book of them lined up for casual visits.

It was the life I'd led. A life I was used to. So why did it hurt so goddamn much to be on the receiving end?

"Okay," I said, forcing a bright smile. "Do you want to skip dinner?"

A tiny frown creased his brow. "No. Do you?"

I didn't. I wanted to spend another few hours with him to top off the incredibly romantic day we'd spent.

But no way in hell was I a glutton for punishment.

"Actually, can we call it quits? It's been a long day and I didn't get much sleep last night."

His eyes narrowed slightly as he stared at me. "I thought that was a good thing?"

"It was, but I'm beat." I faked a yawn. "Thanks for today. It's been amazing."

I could tell he hadn't bought my lame excuse by his deepening frown. But before he could push me further, I slipped out of his embrace.

"You get a head-start on your visit, I'll find my own way home."

He shook his head. "I'll take you home—"

"No," I almost shouted, lowering my voice when several passersby glanced at us. "I'll be fine. See you round."

That's when I did bolt, darting through cars and leaping onto the tram conveniently stopped at traffic lights.

Ash gaped at me but he didn't follow. Instead, he stood rooted to the spot, maintaining eye contact until the tram moved out of sight.

Only then did I allow myself the luxury of letting a few tears fall.

TWELVE
ASHTON

I didn't blame Dani for freaking out.

I was too, but on the inside.

How could I feel so connected to a woman I barely knew?

It wasn't the mind-blowing sex, because I'd had good sex before, but had never felt compelled to be with that person for as long as humanly possible. Yet after last night, that's exactly how I felt about Dani.

Simply, I didn't want to spend the weekend alone.

Despite having a shitload of marking to do—Saturday was my usual catch up day—and a commission to finish, I'd spent the day playing tour guide. And loved every second of it.

Even when she'd been trying on every hat/scarf/brooch/dress in the vintage shops along Brunswick Street, I hadn't been bored. Instead, I'd laughed and teased and been more relaxed than I had been in forever.

There was a lightness to Dani that eased my darkness. And for the first time since we'd met, she'd lost the haunted shadows in her eyes and had appeared genuinely happy.

I knew the feeling, because for those precious hours we spent together? I'd been happy too.

When was the last time I'd been truly happy? When I was a teenager and Mum had regular acting roles? When I'd discovered I could actually earn money for my painting passion? When Mum had a good day and was content to calmly sit and chat about the great times we'd had?

I couldn't remember and it made the hours I'd spent with Dani all the more special.

Then she'd shut down.

One minute we'd been making dinner plans, the next she'd bolted onto that tram without looking back.

I would've liked nothing better to spend another night with her, but the special accom home had rung earlier in the afternoon, saying Mum was having a rare good day if I wanted to visit.

I couldn't say no. And I didn't want to tell Dani the whole story about Mum, so I'd compromised. Dinner before visiting.

But now that visit was over, the best I'd had in a while, and I wanted to see Dani. Wanted to explain. Because the very fact I'd mentioned her to Mum meant she was more than a passing interest.

I may not need the distraction but we'd moved way past that. After last night, it would be even more impossible to get Dani out of my head so the smart thing to do would be discuss where we were at.

Because the friendship she wanted? And the distance I'd wanted? Had combusted in a big way the minute we'd had sex.

I wasn't a complete dickhead. I knew why Dani had shut down. She'd thought I'd been ditching her to visit some other chick. Which meant I had to make a grand gesture and do something I never did: invite her to my place.

I slipped my mobile out of my pocket and fired off a quick text.

WE SKIPPED DINNER SO HOW ABOUT SUPPER AT MY PLACE?

She made me wait a whole ten minutes before responding and in that time I alternated between relieved and manically disappointed.

OK

Short and sweet but I fist-pumped the air.

After firing back my address, I glanced around the tiny two-room bedsit part of a dual occupancy terrace house and wondered what Dani would think.

Though she wasn't snobby in the slightest, she came from A-list Hollywood parents who had mega bucks. Would she take one look at this dive and think I was a loser?

Then my gaze landed on a photo of Mum and I at the Spring Racing Carnival, one of the last functions we'd attended together before the dementia had kicked in hard.

Dani wouldn't have to think anything if I told her the truth. About Mum. About my paintings. About everything.

Was I ready to take that big a risk?

Guess I'd soon find out.

THIRTEEN
DANI

Looked like my stupidity knew no bounds.

I'd run from Ash for one reason.

I was in too deep.

For me to react the way I did over him not wanting to spend the night with me because he had other plans? A huge flashing neon sign that I needed to get a life. One that didn't involve obsessing over the hot Aussie with chocolate brown eyes and a smile that could convince me to do anything.

So rather than ignoring his text message or saying I couldn't make it, I'd spent an inordinate amount of time showering, shaving my legs, lathering body lotion and choosing a suitably casual outfit.

I'd then followed my cell's map instructions to his place, pedaling Clarice like a crazy person.

Yep, definitely stupid.

The more time I spent with Ash, the further I'd fall. That much was obvious. But I wanted to know why he'd cut his visit to the mystery woman short—yeah, I was making a lot of assumptions but it had to be a woman—and if his invitation for supper was because he had an undying need to spend every spare minute with me, like I did with him, or if he just felt guilty for blowing me off earlier.

Either way, I wouldn't get any answers loitering at his front door.

I took a deep breath, released it, and knocked. Didn't surprise me that he lived in a semi-detached house in the back streets of Carlton. Most of the university staff lived close to the campus. But the general disrepair of the place did. The front house looked ready for knockdown and Ash's place didn't look much better. Paint peeled off the weatherboards, moss stained the guttering and the rickety screen door swung on one hinge.

I'd never been hung up on appearances or ownership of things, but to see Ash living like this rammed home how much of a rich bitch I really was. I'd taken so many things for granted growing up. Especially over the last three years, when I'd been content to live off my trust fund and squander cash on a crappy lifestyle. Wasting money on getting wasted. Pathetic.

Yet here was a guy busting his ass working to support his art, content to live in a dump, because there was more to life than designer shoes and A-list parties.

The door opened and I couldn't breathe. Ash had that effect on me. He'd changed into cargo shorts and an olive green T-shirt that molded to his chest. A chest I'd kissed and licked and explored in minute detail.

"Hi," I finally managed, sounding like I'd inhaled helium.

"Glad you came." He ushered me inside and shut the door, like he was afraid I'd run again. "Hungry?"

"Yeah," I said, though food was the furthest thing from my mind.

"Good, because my macaroni and cheese is guaranteed to put hairs on your chest."

"Uh ... okay," I said, not having the faintest idea what he meant.

My clueless expression must've been a giveaway because he laughed. "Means it's hearty."

I swiped my forehead in mock relief. "Phew. You had me worried for a minute."

"Take a seat, I'll dish up and pour the wine." He paused, glanced around the room with a grimace. "We have to eat in here on our laps. Sorry."

"Don't apologize. This place is cozy."

He snorted. "Code for grungy rat hole."

"I like it and want to know why?" I crossed the room in three strides to lay a hand on his shoulder. "Because it's yours and you've let me in."

We both knew I was talking about more than these four walls.

"Back in a sec." He brushed a soft kiss across my lips and I lowered my hand with reluctance.

I needed an anchor because when he kissed me? I definitely swooned a little.

God, I was turning into such a *girl*. If any of the party peeps I hung out with in LA saw me now, they'd think I'd been abducted by aliens and reinserted on earth as a mutant.

Turning my back on that lifestyle hadn't been hard. Trying to make something of my life beyond that was.

And that's what really scared me about my developing relationship with Ash. Was I just hanging around him to take the edge off the constant unsettledness that plagued me? Was I using him?

I'd already fucked up my friendship with Mia, almost to

the point of irrevocability. I'd hate to get in too deep with Ash, only to realize I'd swapped one emotional crutch—booze and drugs—for another.

"Here we go." He re-entered the room, balancing two plates on his arm and holding two wine glass stems in the other.

"Let me guess, you've worked part time as a waiter before."

He nodded. "There's always waiter work in Lygon Street."

"How do you people in Melbourne stay skinny? Between all these incredible foodie streets you have, I'm surprised you're all not this big." I held my arms wide.

"We work it off."

He'd proved just how effective his workout could be last night.

"Wait 'til you see the laneways of the CBD. Best cafés ever." He placed our wine glasses expertly on the table, before taking the plates off his arm.

"Is that an invitation?"

"Only if you're good." His wicked smile indicated he knew exactly how good I could be. "Now, let's eat."

I rarely ate carbs in LA but looked like my new life in Melbourne included pigging out on pasta. I couldn't get enough of the stuff and had to admit, Ash's macaroni and cheese smelled divine.

"So you can cook, huh?" I accepted the plate he offered and my mouth watered, the tantalizing aroma of melted cheese and creamy sauce tickling my nostrils.

"Gourmet all the way." He sat next to me, balancing his plate on his knees. "Macaroni and cheese. Omelets. Salads."

"Bachelor basics 101."

"Uh-huh."

Our conversation stalled as we forked pasta into our mouths. Which was lucky, because his mac and cheese tasted every bit as good as it smelled, and I ended up shoveling the lot into my mouth as fast as I could.

"That was amazing," I said, reaching for my wine at the same time he did. "Compliments to the chef."

I raised my glass in his direction and he clinked it.

"Anytime."

I took a sip of wine. "Considering I've been existing on takeout, I might take you up on that."

Rather than continue our banter, he took my empty plate, stacked it on his and placed them on the cloth-covered coffee table that could be a few crates by the shape.

"Can I ask you something?" He picked up his wine, swirled it around.

I nodded. "Shoot."

"Did you bolt earlier because you thought I was seeing someone else?"

Uh-oh. Not exactly the conversation I wanted to have.

"Look, Ash, we're friends, so who you visit on a Saturday night isn't any of my business and—"

"I was visiting my Mum."

Lucky he couldn't hear my inner whoop of jubilation. Then again, should I be concerned by a guy who'd rather spend a Saturday evening with Mommy than in bed with me?

"She has dementia." He sounded so forlorn I wanted to hug him. "It's not public knowledge so I'd appreciate it if you kept it to yourself."

"My only friend is you so who'd I tell?" Pretty lame joke when he looked so grave.

"It's increasingly rare she has good days, days when she recognizes me, so when the home rang I had to go."

Wow. She was in a home. Which made me feel like a prize bitch for making that sarcastic Mommy comment, even in my own head.

"She's in a home?"

He nodded, worry clouding his eyes. "A special accommodation. She has a room, with round the clock medical care if needed. Meals, activities, and all the therapies onsite." He swirled his wine some more. "It's upmarket, more like a hotel than a home, which I think is important considering she's not that old."

Interesting. When he'd said his mom had dementia, I'd assumed she had Ash late.

As if reading my thoughts, he added, "She's sixty-three. Had me when she was forty." He placed the wine glass on the table. "It's alcohol induced dementia."

"Oh." An inadequate, dumbass response but I didn't know if I should say sorry or not.

"I already told you she was an actress, right?"

I nodded.

"When I came along, surprise of the year, her roles dried up. And I curtailed her party lifestyle." His bitterness was audible. "So not only did her work suffer but her friends weren't around much anymore."

He glanced away, guilt twisting his mouth. "It was a gradual process so by the time I started school, she was partying on her own. A couple of glasses of wine at lunch, a cocktail or two before dinner, a bottle of vodka after."

I touched his hand, trying to convey my support when I knew my words would be inadequate.

"She wasn't drunk all the time. We did loads of fun stuff together and she always had dinner on the table for me every night." He slowly raised his gaze to mine, his pain making me ache to comfort him. "Things got progressively worse in my teens. Her personality changed. One minute she'd be Mum, the next she'd be aggressive and paranoid. She started to forget things, all the time. She couldn't get organized any more, couldn't plan anything, and socially she was a wreck. Then things got really bad when she couldn't learn her lines any more ..."

He shook his head. "It reached a stage two years ago when I couldn't leave her alone in the house for fear she'd harm herself or accidentally burn the place down, so she underwent a full medical assessment and the team recommended she be cared for in a special accom."

I had no idea how the medical system worked in Australia but in the US, if you didn't have insurance, you were screwed. I hoped for Ash's sake that his mom's medical bills were taken care of.

"Sounds like you've both been through a lot."

He nodded, turned his hand over, and threaded his fingers through mine. "I wanted you to know because" —he cleared his throat— "because Mum's a big part of my life. A huge responsibility. So if I rush off to visit her at odd hours it's not because I don't care about you, it's because she may be having a good day and I don't want to miss out on that."

Ash cared about me. He *cared*.

I should be ecstatic. I should be clambering all over him and hugging the life out of him for caring about someone like me.

But all I could think was, no matter how much I wanted this and how much I liked him, being involved with someone as good as Ash could ultimately be bad. For both of us.

Because I knew the closer we got, I'd end up having to tell him the truth and I couldn't bear for him to look at me with derision rather than tenderness.

He squeezed my hand. "Say something."

What could I say, other than I'm the last person he should depend on in any emotional capacity.

But I didn't say that. I couldn't. Not when he was staring at me like he'd just handed me his heart. Which he had in a way, because now I knew about his mom, I knew what made Ash so serious. He had to deal with stuff I barely understood. And by the looks of his home, plus where his mom lived, he probably had financial worries too.

My head said I should leave him alone. He had enough to deal with without getting involved with me.

My heart? Had already rolled over.

"I'll be honest, I was jealous when you said you were visiting someone else tonight. Which pretty much tells me I care about you too." I wrinkled my nose. "But I'm a bad bet, Ash. I'm okay with us having a casual thing while I'm in Melbourne but I'm not a relationship person."

"Good thing I'm not either," he said, with a half-hearted laugh. "But I'll let you in on another secret. I can't remember the last time I had a date. I don't have time for anything other than work and Mum. And I never bring anyone here. So the fact you're here? Speaks volumes."

The way he was staring into my eyes? No words were needed. But I had to ask the one question that was really bugging me, the one I'd never asked anyone else because my expectations had always been low.

"What do you want from me?"

"I want to be with you." He released my hand to cup my face, his thumb softly stroking my bottom lip. "No expectations. No time frames. Just you and me making each other feel good."

Nice in theory but I knew the longer I hung around him, the further I'd fall.

"What do you say?"

I should've said no.

I should've scared him off once and for all by telling him the god-awful truth.

I should've taken a stand before we both got in too deep.

Instead, I closed the short gap between us to whisper against the side of his mouth, "I say yes," a second before I kissed him.

FOURTEEN
DANI

The moment I'd agreed to hang out with Ash, casually or otherwise, I knew this would be inevitable.

Me doing tequila shots in some seedy Melbourne bar with a group of fellow art students I should probably avoid. A small faction of my course that skipped lectures, flunked assignments and partied hard. Very hard.

They were the crew I'd blown off when I'd first started because I'd been there, done that, still detoxing to prove it.

They weren't conducive to my new life: study hard, stay clean and hang out with sensible Ash.

Which is exactly why I was here, downing my fifth shot.

Because hanging out with Ash was scaring the shit out of me.

It had been two weeks since he'd told me about his mom. Two weeks since I'd ended up spending the entire weekend with him. Holed up in his bed. Strolling Carlton hand in hand. Buying gourmet cheese and dips at the Queen Victoria Market. Visiting the zoo. Watching an Aussie Rules footy team train while feeding each other chips and donuts. Doing nauseating couple things that didn't make me feel so sick.

What had I done? Avoided him since. For three long weeks. Been polite via text and email, but determinedly keeping my distance. And when the party crowd asked me out? I accepted. Four times.

The first time I'd avoided a hangover. The second, I'd avoided having sex with the lead singer in a band. The third, I'd avoided accepting a hit of E. The fourth? The night was young.

"So Dani, how hard do you want to par-tay?" Rick, the ringleader of the flunkies, draped an arm over my shoulder. In the past, I would've flirted. Now, he made my skin crawl. "Because our chief supplier just texted me and he'll meet us ASAP. You in?"

It would be so easy to say yes. So easy to lose myself in the mistakes of my past. To slip into a way of life that was easy to forget.

Because ultimately that's what I wanted to do. Forget.

Forget what I'd done. Forget the pain. Forget everything.

"Come on, babe, you know you want to." Rick leaned in close, his lips grazing my ear, and I actually flinched.

"I've got a paper due tomorrow. Rain check?" I shrugged out of his embrace and pasted a bright smile on my face, wondering if the nausea rolling over me was a result of the alcohol I'd imbibed or a result of how he was leering at me.

"I'll hold you to that." He cocked a thumb and forefinger in a gun shape and mock-fired.

Loser.

I made my escape, dodging stumbling patrons and writhing bodies on the dance floor, the boom of the bass reverberating through me.

I'd thrived on this scene once. Had made an art form of scoping the worst guy in the place and going home with him.

I could do it now. Get Ash out of my system once and for all. And start again on my plan for a new life, this time without being plagued by constant doubts: was I stringing him along? Was I doing the right thing? Was I heading for the ultimate fall?

Losing my baby had almost killed me. Several times, if I count the numerous nights I'd woken up in a stranger's house, too wasted to care.

I'd vowed never to allow myself to care about anything or anyone as much again. Because loss was inevitable and the next time, I might not survive.

I stumbled out of the club, knocking over a pole leading to the roped off area.

"Drunk bitch," the bouncer said, glaring at me as he righted it.

I could've taken him on. Could've shoved him, slapped him, or kneed him in the balls. Done that in the past too.

But getting arrested in a foreign country probably wasn't conducive to starting over either, so I walked away. Stood in line for a cab. Took some comfort in the familiarity of my pounding head and the guaranteed oblivion sleep would bring. I'd deal with the inevitable hangover in the morning.

And maybe, just maybe, I'd answer Ash's last text, which he'd sent three days ago.

FIFTEEN
ASHTON

Mum was having a bad day. She didn't know who I was but she seemed to enjoy hearing my voice. So I'd read the newspaper and a chapter of a historical romance, the books she used to devour when I was growing up.

Now she was staring off into space and I was about to leave when she said, "You have an excellent tone. I knew an actor who sounded like you once." She turned her head slowly, her gaze vacant as she glanced past me. "Talk to me."

So I did. Mindless chatter, really, about the latest batch of students I was tutoring, the commission I was working on for a wealthy Toorak family, and Dani.

Initially I rambled, but when it came to Dani, it sounded like I was voicing my innermost fears.

"This girl is driving me nuts. First she chases me, then she ignores me for weeks."

"Maybe she wants you to chase her." Mum fiddled with the cotton fringe of the scarf wrapped around her bony shoulders. "Some girls like playing hard to get."

"Not this one. She seems more open than that."

Then again, what did I know? Dani had secrets, I knew that. She shut down at times and had this look in her eye ... half-fear, half-defiance, like she was daring life to kick her butt and she'd kick right back.

"You should try romancing her. Girls like that." Mum's wistful sigh echoed. "We like to be appreciated."

I wanted to hug her. To tell her she was, that I'd never forget the bond we shared and how much she'd given up to have me. But physical contact scared her when she didn't know who I was, so I crossed my arms to stop from reaching for her.

"So you think flowers and chocolates, huh?"

Mum snorted. "Why do men always think it takes all that fluff to impress a woman, when all we really need is a little attention?"

I smiled, impressed that even with dementia my mum made more sense than some of the immature students I dealt with on a daily basis.

"Young man, it's simple. Turn up at her house. Ask her to go for a walk." Her gaze clouded. "I used to love going for walks with my boyfriends."

"Okay, I'll do that." I stood and held out my hand, hoping the sadness seeping through me didn't show.

I hated this part. Hated that she didn't know who I was. Hated that I couldn't hug her. Hated that I'd be lucky if she shook my hand.

"Thanks for stopping by." After a long pause, she placed her hand in mine for an all-too-brief moment. "And good luck with your girl."

"Thanks." I cleared my throat, the inevitable rush of emotion making me choke up. "I'll let you know how I get on."

"I'll look forward to it." Her eyelids drifted shut as I backed out of the room, wishing things were different. Wishing Mum was her old self. Wishing for a lot of things.

But Mum used to say wishes were futile, if you wanted something done you needed to go out there and make it happen.

With Dani, that's exactly what I intended to do.

∽

"YOU'RE AVOIDING ME." I stood on Dani's doorstep, drinking in the sight of her in denim shorts and a red tank top, resisting the urge to back her into the hallway, kick the door shut and take her up against the nearest wall.

"Been busy," she said, leaning against the door but not inviting me in.

"Aren't we all."

Increasingly perplexed by her cool attitude, I said the first thing that popped into my head. "Want to take a walk?"

Her eyebrows rose as one, like it was the last thing she expected to hear. "Where to?"

"Some of my favorite inner city haunts."

I loved the laneways of the inner city, narrow cobbled streets jam-packed with cafés, restaurants, galleries and boutiques. People sat out on the street any time of day or night, and I'd spent many hours just sitting and sketching, trying to capture the vibe down on paper to paint later.

I'd planned a whole series around laneway life and would love to finish what I'd started. If I ever got time to paint for pleasure rather than money again.

Dani shuffled, one bare foot rubbing against the other. "I've got a ton of homework to do—"

"Fine. Just forget it."

I was done. We hadn't seen each other in three weeks and if this was the reception I got, I'd rather be anywhere but here. We'd agreed to keep things casual, but Dani was taking that to extremes.

I didn't need this. I thought we'd connected on a level deeper than sex. I'd been wrong.

I was halfway down the path before she spoke. "Sorry."

I stopped and turned back. "Sorry for what? For not being polite enough to answer my texts? For blowing hot and cold? For shutting me down after I take the time to visit on the off-chance you may actually want to hang out together?"

Her eyes widened to saucer-proportions, huge orbs of blue that made my resolve to leave falter. She looked so lost, so bleak, I had to dig my heels in to stop from running toward her and holding her tight.

"Sorry for all of it." She stepped outside and lingered on the porch step. "You're a good guy, Ash. You don't need someone like me in your life."

"Whoa, where did that come from?" I held up my hands. "Firstly, I thought we already agreed to be friends. Secondly, I don't *need* anyone but I like to hang out with people who matter to me. And lastly, you're the most interesting woman I've met in ages, so maybe I do need someone like you."

I could've sworn her lower lip wobbled. Shit, that's all I needed, to make her cry.

"You could've said I was captivating or mesmerizing or intriguing rather than boring old interesting."

"Do I look like a fucking greeting card?"

She finally smiled and the transformation was incredible. She morphed from nervous and recalcitrant to warm and glowing. "If your offer still stands, I'd like to take a walk with you."

I shrugged, like her acceptance meant little, when in fact I was punching the air in victory on the inside. "Sure, I'll wait out here."

She jerked a thumb over her shoulder. "You could wait inside?"

No, I couldn't. Because if I set foot inside her flat after not seeing her, not touching her, for three weeks, I knew exactly what would happen and it wouldn't involve walking.

"I'll give you five minutes." I held up my hand, fingers spread. "The laneways wait for no woman."

"Fine, I'll be out in three." She bounded up the steps, leaving me a tantalizing view of her sensational arse. Which I'd grabbed and caressed and nipped ... like that was helping.

As if it wasn't bad enough I'd spent every spare second, and many working ones too, over the last three weeks replaying what we'd done. And adding a bit more, ramping up the fantasies until it's all I could think about.

I hadn't expected to feel like this after our time apart. I felt ... whole. Like I'd been drifting along and being with her made me feel complete somehow.

Crazy, considering we weren't seriously dating and had only known each other less than two months. But there was something about Dani that made me feel good. Like I recognized a kindred spirit. Someone as lost as I was. Someone who needed to be guided through all the crap that life threw our way.

"Let's go." She locked up and walked toward me, her long legs eliciting memories of how they'd felt wrapped around me. "Though if you keep looking at me like that, maybe we should stay in?"

"Nope, we're walking," I said, holding out my hand, wondering if she'd take it, pathetically relieved when she did. "What have you been up to? Apart from ignoring me, that is."

"Lectures. Assignments. Partying." She almost threw the last word out defiantly, like she expected I'd judge her.

"That's great. You should blow off steam with friends in a new city."

She didn't speak but I sensed a sideways glance, as if she were sizing me up.

"You're not mad I've ignored you yet hung out with others?"

Mad? No. Disappointed? A little. Stupid, because we'd made it more than clear what we were to each other, but there was a small part of me deep down that was plain old jealous at the thought of others getting to hang out with her instead of me.

"We're not joined at the hip, so you hang out with whoever you like."

I was trying to be magnanimous but I knew I'd said the wrong thing when her hand went slack in mine.

I stopped and turned to face her. "What do you want me to say, Dani? That I missed you? That I can't stop thinking about you? That while these last few weeks have been manically busy for me, I would've made time for you if you'd let me?"

She opened her mouth to respond, closed it again, shook her head. "I don't want to get too involved, you know that."

So it was back to this.

"Yeah, I do. I also know that we've been over this. So

what has you in such a funk that you've avoided me for weeks?"

She glanced away, worrying her bottom lip with her teeth, before she finally murmured, "I already like you too much."

That's the best thing I'd heard all day. But something was bugging her and I knew I'd have to get to the bottom of it if we were to move forward and enjoy this evening.

"And that's a bad thing because?"

"Because I don't handle goodbyes well." She dragged her gaze back to mine, her gloominess surprising. "What's the point of dating when it's going to end anyway?"

I tugged on her hands, bringing her closer to me. "The point is, we live in the moment. We don't worry what may happen tomorrow or next week or four months from now when you head back to the States. We just live."

I released her hands to rest mine on her waist. "Seeing my mum deteriorate has taught me that if nothing else."

"How is she?"

"The same. Up and down. Mostly down." I smiled. "But she did encourage me to go after you."

Dani blinked, several times. "You told her about me?"

I nodded. "Yeah, but it's no biggie. She didn't know who I was at the time."

The corners of her mouth curved upward. "You're pretty amazing."

"Yeah, so amazing I have to practically beg you to hang out with me."

She paused, tilted her head slightly, studying me. "So you reckon I should live in the moment, huh?"

"Yep."

"Then come with me." She snagged my hand off her

waist and started walking. In the opposite direction we'd been headed, retracing our steps.

"Where are we going?"

"My place." Her eyes twinkled with mischief. "The laneways of Melbourne can wait. Me? I'm not so patient."

That made two of us as we practically sprinted all the way back to her flat.

SIXTEEN
DANI

I'd just had the most incredible weekend of my life.

If the last time I'd hung out with Ashton had been romantic, this weekend topped that.

When we'd made it back to my place last night, we hadn't left my bed until one PM today. We'd made it our own private party for two, ordering in Chinese between bouts of sensational sex.

The only reason why we'd left our cozy cocoon was so he could show me his beloved laneways. And I had to admit they were cool. Not quite as cool as being tucked away with Ash under the quilt for a sex marathon, but cool nonetheless.

We'd strolled Hosier Lane and Hardware Lane and Block Arcade, and were now nursing steaming hot cocoas in Degraves Street, people watching.

"Do you come here often?"

He chuckled. "Babe, we're way past the pick-up line."

I rolled my eyes. "You seem really at home here." I trailed my fingertip down his cheek. "I've never seen you look so animated."

He shrugged, like my observation meant little, but I saw the way he looked at me before he glanced away: like he couldn't believe we were so in sync after hardly spending any time together. That made two of us.

"I come here for inspiration." He pointed to a café opposite. "That's my favorite place. I could spend hours there, watching and sketching."

"And eating." I pushed my plate away, having been indoctrinated into the pleasures of the vanilla slice, solid custard between two slivers of pastry, topped with icing. An Aussie staple apparently. One that was way too addictive. "Have you painted this laneway?"

Some of his excitement faded as shadows clouded his eyes. "No."

"Why not, if you love it so much?"

"Because I don't have the time," he snapped, his lips compressing into a thin line.

Oo-kay. Guess I'd touched a nerve.

"Sorry." He pinched the bridge of his nose, as if staving off a headache. "I've got a ton of ideas, mainly thanks to this place, but doing commissions doesn't leave me much spare time."

I bit back my first response, one that my last nanny used to constantly say. 'If you don't have time, make time.' Easy for her to say, when she was being paid an exorbitant sum by the hour.

Ash stirred sugar into his latte. "I've got a series planned. One I'd like to ultimately show in a gallery."

"Wow, that's great. You should totally do it," I said, eager to take a look at what this wonderful, brooding guy could produce. I bet his art would be as deep as him. Intense. "Do you have somewhere lined up? Because I'm so there—"

"Thanks for the vote of confidence, but I need to

complete a series of paintings before I can even approach galleries." He covered my hand with his. "I owe you an apology."

"What for?"

"Because when I lobbed on your doorstep yesterday, I accused you of blowing me off for the last three weeks, when in reality I've been so flat out I couldn't have seen you if I wanted to." He grimaced. "Between working at uni, visiting Mum and doing the commissions, I don't have much time left over for painting let alone a girlfriend."

I froze. Girlfriend. The one label that struck fear into my heart.

I'd never been anyone's girlfriend. I didn't want to be anyone's girlfriend. Because that kind of attachment came with huge risks.

So I fell back on my tried and true method when something made me uncomfortable. Deflect.

"Careful there, Mister. Don't go throwing that girlfriend tag around so freely." I forced a laugh.

By the speed in which he removed his hand from mine, it didn't work.

"We're casual, Dani, I get it. But you're a girl. And a friend. So don't get hung up over it." He sounded hurt, and more than a little bitter.

Time for some serious backpedaling and that involved revealing far more than I was ready for. "It's not you, it's me."

He raised his eyebrows at my cliché, so I rushed on. "I've never had a relationship. They freak me out. I don't like co-dependence. I don't like obligations."

"Relationships can also be fun and easygoing with the right person."

God, he sounded so trite. Sure, it must be tough seeing

his mom deteriorate mentally before his eyes but what did Ash know about real pain, real loss, and the very real agony of saying goodbye to a baby that never was.

"Let me guess. You've left a trail of broken hearts."

He shook his head. "Not quite. One serious relationship in high school, we went out for two years. But then Mum started going downhill ..."

He left the rest unsaid. Ash may not know about loss but by his audible pain every time he mentioned his mom, he'd done it tough.

While I'd spent the last three years partying my way around LA to forget, he'd been devoting his life to work and his sick mom. We were poles apart. So why did being with him feel so goddamn right?

I laid my hand on his thigh. "If I was girlfriend material, you'd be the only candidate for the job of boyfriend."

His kissable mouth eased into a smile that made my chest ache. "You already got the girl-friend position the first moment I saw you."

I melted. "Bullshit. You were grumpy I'd run you over."

"Nah, just angling for the sympathy vote." He slid an arm around my waist and pulled me close. "Considering you're still hanging out with me a couple months later, it must've worked."

I elbowed him, laughing when he mock winced. "Guess you didn't get the message when I didn't respond to your texts."

His arm around my waist loosened its grip a little. "And what message is that?"

That I was terrified of how he made me feel.

That I was in way over my head already.

That I was crazy-angry at myself for breaking my do-over rule and falling for a guy on my first night in Melbourne.

But I didn't say any of it, settling for a half-truth. "I didn't respond to your texts because I'm struggling." And not just with college. "Being an older student is tough. I feel like a dork for not knowing half the stuff I'm supposed to. And you're a major distraction, one I can't afford if I'm to make a success of this."

"Answering someone's text messages shouldn't be such a big distraction," he said, sounding less angry now I'd stroked his ego.

"You're the distraction." I poked him in the chest. "And you know it."

"Me?" He squared his shoulders and puffed out his chest, as I laughed at his false modesty.

"Yeah, you." I jabbed him in the chest again for good measure. "When we hang out like this, it just feels so amazing, so right. And it's all I can think about afterward, so yeah, it messes with my head."

I hadn't meant to reveal so much but I had to make him understand why I'd acted like a bitch over the whole girlfriend thing.

Because Ash's opinion mattered to me. What he thought of me mattered. He *mattered* to me.

"Know the feeling." He brushed a soft kiss across my lips and that weird half-moan came from me. "So what do two people who can't afford any distractions do when they're crazy about each other?"

I wanted to say 'I'm not crazy about you' but I was done lying for the day. This weekend would end all too soon and we'd go back to our respective lives: him juggling responsibilities, me trying to forget. Everything.

"We make the most of the time we have together."

Sounded like such a simple solution when in fact it was anything but. Because for me, I had no intention of spending more weekends like this with Ash.

Everything between us was so ... intimate. In and out of the bedroom. I'd never had a physical connection with any guy that wasn't transient and designed to make me forget for a few hours. With Ash, I wanted to remember everything we did in erotic detail.

Then there was this: the handholding, the hugging, the city exploring, the talking. Real couple stuff. But the only real thing for us was our inevitable goodbye when I headed back to the US.

"Does that mean you'll respond to my texts?"

I tapped him on the nose. "Only if you're lucky."

"I'm feeling very lucky." He leaned in to nuzzle my neck. "And about to get luckier if we head back to your place."

"Cocky too." I playfully shoved him away, already half-standing.

He left a few bills on the table and snagged my hand. "Let's go make the most of our time together."

I didn't need to be asked twice.

SEVENTEEN
DANI

Not surprising, I went out every night for the next two weeks after my weekend with Ash.

I missed three deadlines, two study dates and an appointment to discuss my grades with a senior lecturer.

Worse than my perpetual hangover was the fact I didn't care.

Ironic, I'd finally met a guy who could help me outrun my past but I'd stopped fleeing. I didn't need Ash's help. I didn't need Ash. Much easier to self-sabotage and prove what I'd always known.

I was a big fucking failure.

Something that was categorically proved when I sorted through a stack of unopened mail and tore open an envelope from the uni. An envelope bearing the results of my first semester.

I scanned the subjects and associated grades, and let the numbness wash over me.

I'd barely passed two subjects. Out of six.

I crumpled the paper into a ball and flung it at the trash.

Yeah, like that would erase the evidence of exactly how much of a failure I was.

Looked like I couldn't do anything right. Relationships. Family. Study. I was hopeless at all of it.

How the hell did I think for one minute I could leave my past behind? Leaving LA hadn't done a damn thing for my new start. It was pretty obvious I could run to the ends of the earth and I'd be just as much of a loser there.

Feeling sick to my stomach, I picked up my cell and scrolled through the contacts. So far, I'd sought oblivion in alcohol only, but seeing the cold, hard evidence of my new life in tatters meant I needed something more. The mindless nothingness that could only be achieved by chemical enhancement.

I found Rick's number and my thumb hovered over the call button. I had no idea why I was hesitating. I hadn't in the past, when I could go for days trying to forget the mess I'd made of my life. I liked not thinking, not remembering, not blaming.

Because for those few blissful hours when I was mentally floating in some euphoric place devoid of sorrow, I could almost believe I was normal. That I wasn't some perpetual sad-case that craved attention so much I'd gone to extremes and killed my baby in the process.

My laptop beeped at that moment, indicating an incoming Skype call.

Could only be one person.

Mia.

I glanced between the screen and the cell in my hand, torn. Mia would take one look at my face and know I was a mess. Easier to shut down the laptop, call Rick and set about forgetting. Everything.

But then I remembered what had driven me here in the

first place. How I'd deliberately alienated my best friend and the only person in this world who truly cared about me. How much I'd hurt her. How I'd nearly ruined her first real relationship and ours in the process.

I'd hit rock-bottom when I'd sabotaged Mia and Kye's relationship and that had ultimately been the catalyst to start over here in Melbourne.

And what was I doing? About to screw up all over again because I was in one of my classic downward spirals.

The laptop screen beeped again, sounding more insistent this time and with a yell that was half-rage, half-frustration, I flung my cell onto the couch.

Stabbing at the Skype button, I dragged the laptop toward me and settled into a saggy armchair as Mia's face popped onto the screen.

"Hey Dani. Did I screw up the time differences? Were you asleep? Sorry, I just had to chat and see how you're doing."

Typical Mia, her enthusiasm for life bubbling over so much she rambled. Made me realize how much I missed her. And how much I'd almost lost when I hurt her.

"I wasn't asleep." I forced a smile, hoping she couldn't gauge my fragility from a million miles away. "How are you?"

"Great. Really great." She glanced over her shoulder, at her dorm door in the background. "Kye's just gone to get us some snacks while we study."

She squealed and clapped her hands. "Can you believe he's actually here? I'm so lucky."

Yeah, she was. My eternally optimistic friend who only saw the good in people had met a guy who worshipped her. I envied her that. It's one of the reasons I'd tried to fuck it up for her. Guess I was a jealous bitch as well as a loser.

"Anyway, enough about me," she said, pointing at the screen. "Tell me about you."

Hoping I could pull off the biggest con of the century, I shrugged. "Not much to tell. I'm studying hard. Seeing the touristy stuff in Melbourne. Meeting new people."

Mia hesitated, and I knew why. She wanted to ask if I was dating, if there was a guy in my life. Because it's what I'd done in the past, constantly boasting about my conquests. She'd hated it and deep down, I had too. Making myself out to be worse of a slut than I was hadn't helped my self-esteem. It may have garnered me some attention but at what cost? My reputation had been shitty. And toward the end in LA, I'd done my utmost to live up to it.

"Have you found a hot Aussie to rival Kye?"

"Maybe." The word popped out before I could censure it. Damn.

Mia leaned forward, peering into the screen. "Ooh, tell me more. What's he like?"

"He's serious and determined and very cute. Works as a tutor at the university, but he's an artist too," I said, the truth tumbling out in a rush. "We've hung out a few times. Had meals together. Toured the city. That kind of thing. And he's the first guy I've really connected with, you know."

Mia nodded. "I know, sweetie. And I'm so glad you've met someone. He sounds amazing."

"He is."

"But?" A tiny frown appeared between Mia's brows.

"But what?"

Mia sighed. "I can see something's drastically wrong, Dani. I've seen you look like this before."

Increasingly defensive, I folded my arms. "When?"

"After one of your all-night benders." Mia paused, glanced away, before pinning me with an accusatory stare.

"You said you were starting afresh in Melbourne. That you weren't going to get wasted anymore. What happened?"

"Ashton happened," I murmured, wishing we were having this conversation face to face and not through a computer interface. "He's too good for me. He's dedicated and sweet and so focused he makes me look like a flake. Plus there's no future for us as I'll be leaving in a few months. So what's the point?"

She shook her head. "The point is, sounds like you've got a wonderful guy who likes you, so you're reverting to type and doing your damndest to push him away."

"Bullshit—"

"You've run from emotional commitment your whole life, sweetie. You want attention but you're terrified when you get it. I understand, I really do. But there comes a point when you need to make a stand for what you really want." Mia touched the screen. "That time for you is now."

I shook my head, tears blurring my eyes. "You know what I'm like. I'll only fuck up his life and mine. I'm not dependable—"

"Stop right there."

I jumped, having never heard Mia use that tone with me before. She sounded seriously angry; and cold, like she had in the aftermath of when I'd made a play for Kye to hurt her.

"You need to stop self-destructing out of guilt or you'll end up crazy ..." Mia paused, looked me straight in the eye, and said, " ... or dead."

Wow, my sweet, malleable friend had grown a backbone while I'd been away. And I liked it. She was saying the stuff I needed to hear. Because the way I was feeling now? And how close I'd come to calling Rick for a hit? I was in deep shit, in a place I'd vowed never to return to.

In that moment, I wished I was back home, surrounded by the familiar, able to crawl into my own bed, pull the covers up and hide away for a week, just like I'd done after I'd miscarried.

Seeing Mia, talking to her, only served to increase my homesickness and I swallowed the sobs that threatened to burst out of me in a loud, angry wail.

"I've been partying hard with a crowd from university. No drugs though. Trying to forget how much I want to be with Ashton all the time. Trying to stop wanting him so much. And now I'm flunking on top of everything else ..." I shook my head and took a deep breath, drowning in self-pity. "I feel like I've failed all over again. Failed at my do-over, my studies, everything."

"You need to cut yourself some slack, sweetie," Mia said, her tone soft and understanding. "You've undertaken some massive changes and topped those off with a move to a new country. Give yourself a break."

I was. That's what letting Ash in had been about. He'd brought something into my life, an optimism, that had been missing for so long. But he'd done such a good job of making me feel whole again that I'd freaked and pushed him away, even if he didn't know it yet.

Maybe that's what I should do. Show him the real me. The girl who partied hard and long, who lived life in the moment, who didn't care about sucky grades.

"I'll be okay." I forced a bright smile, knowing Mia would see through it. "I knew first semester would be the toughest, adjusting to studying again. It'll just take time to get on top of things."

It all sounded so logical. Pity I hadn't acknowledged the truth earlier.

"College, sure. But what about Ashton? What are you going to do about him?"

Fucked if I knew.

Ashton would be perfect boyfriend material. And even though we'd deliberately spelled out our relationship as not boyfriend/girlfriend, that's exactly how we behaved toward one another.

But I didn't want a boyfriend. I didn't need a boyfriend. Now if only my susceptible heart could believe it.

"We'll continue to hang out occasionally."

Mia's eyes narrowed. "Isn't that what you're doing now? Doesn't seem to be working out so well."

"That's because I'm an idiot, going against my initial plan to stay away from guys and falling for one regardless."

Mia's eyebrows shot up. "You've fallen for him?"

I could deny it but what would be the point? Talking to Mia had calmed me down and prevented me from doing something monumentally dumb, like scoring from Rick. She'd always been my voice of reason and I needed her objectivity now more than ever.

"Yeah, I like him. A lot."

Mia mouthed 'wow'.

"I know, crazy, huh? Me, pining for a guy?" I twisted the end of my ponytail around my finger. "But I know this can't go anywhere and I don't want to end up hurting as bad as when I lost ..."

Not that I could compare breaking up with a boyfriend to losing my baby, but the only other time I'd become attached to someone so quickly was with the baby. And I was still grieving three years later.

No way in hell I wanted to be pining after Ash when I went back to LA.

Mia gnawed on her bottom lip, as if she didn't want to

speak, before she sat up straighter. "Have you ever thought of seeing someone to deal with your issues?"

I shook my head. "I don't do shrinks."

"Grief counselor?"

"You can't grieve for someone you never had." I was a big, fat liar as well as a failure, because that's exactly what I'd been doing for years.

"Oh sweetie, this is me you're talking to." She pressed her palm to the screen again. "I care about you and I don't want to leave you when you're like this."

"I'm fine." If I forced this fake smile much longer, my face would set in rigor mortis. "Seriously. Seeing you made me a tad homesick, you know? And it's that time of the month, so don't mind me. You know I'm a survivor."

A deep frown creased Mia's brow. "Promise you'll call or Skype me any time, day or night, if you need me?"

I nodded. "Promise." Childish, but I crossed my fingers under the table.

"Okay, I've got to go. Take care." Mia blew a kiss at the screen.

"You too, babe." I quickly closed the laptop screen before I burst into tears.

The only other time Mia had seen me cry was when I'd apologized for coming onto Kye and told her about the baby. If she saw me cry now, she'd know how truly on the edge I was.

My gaze fell on the crumpled piece of paper, as tattered as my grades. Kye's dad had called in favors to get me into Melbourne University at such short notice. Being a mega TV talk show host in Australia, he had friends everywhere apparently.

What if one of those friends at the university let him

know how bad I was failing? Would the news make its way back to Kye and Mia?

Shit, I couldn't risk it.

Apart from being exceedingly ungrateful to screw up this chance, I had a constant niggling fear that if I couldn't make it here, I couldn't make it anywhere and I'd revert to my old life when I returned to the States.

The old life I was semi-replicating already.

I let loose a frustrated yell and snatched up my cell, deleting Rick from my contacts.

If my shocking grades hadn't been enough of a wake up call, the disappointment in Mia's eyes when she'd seen my hung-over state gave me the kick in the ass I needed.

I had to get back on track.

Starting now.

EIGHTEEN
ASHTON

I'd been deluding myself.

All these weeks away from Dani I'd believed my self-talk. Almost. Stuff like we could keep this casual, that I'd be satisfied with the occasional text message or phone call, that we were friends.

Bullshit. All of it.

Because the fact was, I couldn't stop thinking about her, couldn't stop wanting to be with her.

That wasn't a sign of a guy doing casual.

That was a sign of a guy wanting way more.

Which was crazy, considering how different we were. While my waking hours were consumed by work and Mum, Dani was indulging in the perfect uni life: lectures and assignments tempered with non-stop socializing.

I'd heard on the grapevine she'd been hanging out with the party crowd every night. Admittedly, I'd been pissed off, before realizing just because I'd never had the time to socialize didn't mean other students were the same.

Dani was a bright, intelligent, attractive woman, with a killer Californian accent. Stood to reason she'd be at the heart of any party. And so she should be. She'd admitted to enjoying that lifestyle back home and dabbling here, only a matter of time before she felt comfortable enough here to hang out with the in-crowd.

So I'd quashed my jealousy and let her have her space. I hadn't contacted her much and to my annoyance, she'd done the same. Didn't stop me wondering every second of every day what she was doing and who she was doing it with.

Which brought me to tonight.

As much as I hated the party lifestyle after I'd seen what it did to Mum, if I wanted to be a part of Dani's life, I'd have to compromise.

I'd showed her the parts of Melbourne I loved. Now it was time to do things her way.

She walked into the pub at that moment and my heart twisted. Yeah, real casual. Not.

I stood and her face lit up when she caught sight of me. Heads turned as she wound her way through the crowd, watching the tall blonde in tight denim and a pink T-shirt, and who could blame them.

Dani was a knockout. And I wanted to make her all mine.

Time to stop stuffing around. Tonight, I'd show her I could act my age and have fun like the rest of the crowd, and hopefully make her see I wanted more than friendship, despite everything I'd said to the contrary.

"Hey, you." She kissed me on my cheek, a friendly greeting she'd give anyone and I tried not to let my disappointment show. "Long time no see."

"Too long," I said, silently cursing when I sounded too flippant. "I missed you."

"That's sweet." She actually patted my hand as she sat on the stool next to me. "Beer?"

I nodded. "Please." While inside, I was dying a slow death. No 'I missed you too.' No sign that we'd had mind-blowing sex, albeit weeks ago. No sign that she was interested in me as anything other than a friend.

Had I left my run too late? Had Dani hooked up with someone else?

"I didn't think you were the pub crawl type," she said, dragging her gaze upward to meet my eyes, but not before I'd glimpsed her staring longingly at my mouth.

Maybe all was not lost.

"I'm not, but we haven't hung out in ages and I know you're into this, so here I am." I picked up the beer the waiter had just deposited and raised it. "Here's to us."

She hesitated and for one god-awful moment I thought she wouldn't toast. "To us," she finally said, lightly clinking her beer bottle to mine.

Damn, I had to play this right. Showing my feelings too soon could make her bolt, considering we hadn't seen each other in a while. I needed to take things slow, work up to telling her the truth: that I was through doing the casual friendship thing and I wanted to date. For real.

"So how many pubs constitute a crawl? Three?"

She laughed. "Try eight, my friend. And you have to drink in all of them."

"I'm a lightweight these days. Four of these?" I tapped my beer bottle. "And I'll be blind."

"I'll look after you." She winked and took a long swig of beer, while I could do was stare helplessly at the elegant column of her neck and quell the urge to nip her there.

"What have you been up to?" Wouldn't bode well to

mention I already knew she'd been partying up a storm. Screamed stalker.

"The usual. Studying. Going out. You know how it is."

Actually, I didn't. Because all I'd ever done as an undergrad was study, paint and look after Mum.

She touched my hand and I swear my skin sizzled. "How about you?"

I shrugged. "Same old, same old."

We lapsed into an awkward silence and I silently cursed for leaving things so long between us.

"Do you want to check out the usual student haunts or try a few new bars?"

She stilled for a moment and looked away, as if I'd said the wrong thing. "I'd prefer seeing new bars."

"Okay. Ready to hit the next?" I downed the rest of my beer, eager to be on the move and hopefully work off this stiltedness between us.

"Sure." She slid off the stool and I noticed she'd barely touched her beer. "Let's go."

I took her hand and thankfully she didn't pull free. We dodged our way through the rowdy crowd and all I could think was how much I'd love to ditch the pub-crawl and take Dani back to my place.

On the rare times I did go out, I didn't miss the sticky carpet from years of beer spills, the alcohol haze that hung over the patrons like a pall, the smell of stale cigarette smoke and the general sleaziness.

I didn't want to spend the next few hours in dives like this. I wanted Dani, naked and warm in my arms.

But as she tugged me forward and we finally made it out onto the street, I knew I'd do whatever it took, including endure a night of trawling pubs, to be with this woman on a more permanent basis for whatever time we had left.

NINETEEN
DANI

I knew I was in trouble the moment I entered the fourth bar.

Usually, I'd thrive on discovering new places to drown my sorrows. It gave me a buzz: scoping out the crowd, trying new drinks, losing myself in the music.

Tonight was different. And not just because I had an amazing guy by my side, being supportive and fun.

Simply, the gloss had worn off.

Somewhere between Mia's Skype call and nursing my third drink of the night at the third pub—usually I would've downed four at each place—I'd realized that this wasn't working anymore.

I wasn't feeling the usual buzz. Wasn't having fun. Wasn't forgetting.

Yet when I was with Ash, it didn't matter.

Having him hold my hand, talking to me, listening to me, meant I didn't have to drown out the pain that constantly plagued me. That insistent little voice inside my head that chanted 'you're a loser. You killed your baby. You're the reason no-one loves you.'

When Mia had suggested I see a shrink, I hadn't told her I already had. I'd been going a little nuts after I miscarried and had seen a psychologist a few times. Not one of the Beverly Hills shrinks frequented by my folks and their fake friends, but a woman in Venice Beach. She'd looked like a hippy, smelled like incense, sounded like a chain-smoker, but she'd been a lifesaver.

She'd let me talk. And talk. And talk. I'd spilled so many secrets with her I'd been a goddamned sieve. The best part, she hadn't lectured or judged. She'd let me problem solve. Too bad once I stopped seeing her I chose other methods to numb the pain.

"You okay?"

I faked a yawn. "A bit tired."

Ash's eyes crinkled when he smiled. "Don't tell me your party animal reputation is crap."

"Been a long week." Been a long few months and I was finally realizing I couldn't keep doing what I was doing.

Something had to give. As long as it wasn't my sanity.

"Do you mind if we call it a night?"

He nodded, his smile fading. "I'll take you home."

He said it hesitantly, like he half expected I'd refuse.

"Thanks, that'd be great." I slid my hand into his. "I'd like to talk."

"Uh-oh. That sounds bad."

"Actually, it's good." At least, I hoped it would be. "Thanks for tonight. I know it's not your scene." I kissed him on the cheek, surprisingly chaste when all I'd wanted to do all night was pash him silly.

"What gave it away? My walking stick or earplugs?"

I laughed. "You're not that old."

He cupped his hand behind his ear. "Pardon? This music has made me deaf."

I nudged him with my elbow. "Come on, let's get out of here."

The moment we stepped out into the crisp Melbourne air, I took a deep breath. Even though we were in the CBD, this city's air was cleaner than LA on a good day.

"I'll miss this when I leave." I released a breath, took another.

"This?" He swung our linked hands high. "You and me?"

"I meant the fresh air, but this too." I squeezed his hand when he lowered it. "Actually, that's what I want to talk about."

"Me too." He turned to face me, his expression somber. "I know we said it's not worth starting something serious because we're too busy and you're leaving. But I've changed my mind."

He released my hand, to step in closer and slide his arms around my waist. "I want us to be in a relationship, for whatever time we have together. I know we've got commitments elsewhere, but I reckon we can make this work. What do you think?"

I wanted to say yes. I wanted to shout it to the world how a guy as incredible as Ash could want to be with me.

But every, old insecurity I'd ever had reared up, plaguing me with familiar doubts. The main one being, was I good enough?

"I think you're amazing, but ..."

He stiffened, tension bracketing his mouth. "But what?"

"But what if I let you down? I'm unreliable and fickle and self-absorbed. I haven't had a relationship before, I wouldn't know how." I puffed out my cheeks. "And I suck at emotionally connecting with anyone."

"Well, when you put it like that ..." The corners of his mouth curved into a devastating smile that made all that fresh air catch in my lungs. "Don't overanalyze this. Trust what you feel in here." He placed a hand above my left breast, over my heart. "I think we'd be good together."

In the end, it was as simple as that.

Because I didn't think we'd be good together. I thought we'd be frigging great together.

"Guess I have my first boyfriend," I said, beaming at him like a lunatic.

"Guess you do." He kissed me, hard and fast, and I combusted.

It was like that between us. Maybe because of the time since we'd last seen each other, maybe it was good old-fashioned pheromones, but whenever we kissed it was like the first time. Passionate and frantic and oh-so-hot.

When we eased apart, he rested his forehead against mine. "Want to hear something funny?"

"What?"

"I think I'm drunk." He straightened and held up both hands, fingers extended, thumb down on one hand. "I've had three drinks at each bar, so that's nine in total."

I laughed. "So you wouldn't have made that grand declaration if you'd been sober?"

He swooped in for another kiss. "It's all I've been thinking about for weeks so yeah, I would've gone all soppy sober too."

I tapped my bottom lip, pretending to think. "If you're drunk, does that mean I get to take advantage of you?"

"Hell yeah." He held his arms wide. "Have your wicked way with me. Do your worst, babe."

I stepped into his arms and when he wrapped them around me, I'd never felt so cherished. "Lucky for you, it'll only be the best."

We couldn't board a tram fast enough.

TWENTY
ASHTON

I hadn't had a hangover this bad since I was fourteen and had drunk an entire bottle of ouzo to keep up with my mates.

Not that I was a teetotaler these days, but I didn't have time to go out drinking and I didn't have a hell of a lot of spare cash to spend on alcohol.

So those nine drinks last night? Had given me one mother of a headache. Combined with the dry mouth and the queasiness? Thank God I wouldn't have to do it again anytime soon to impress Dani.

I rolled over in bed to watch her sleep and a rush of something so strong, so powerful, made me gasp like I'd been sucker-punched.

I cared for this woman.

More than I'd ever cared about anyone, discounting Mum.

And it terrified me.

Because now that I'd opened myself up to the possibility of more than friendship, I knew I'd get in too deep. Which meant inevitable pain when she left.

But I could handle it, because if there was one thing I'd learned watching Mum deteriorate, it was to make the most of every moment. I'd seen that old cliché life was too short proved before my very eyes and no way did I want to regret not having a relationship with Dani because it had an expiry date.

Dani slept, oblivious to my goofy grin as I watched her lips purse, emitting tiny puffs of air, while her eyelids fluttered occasionally. She had a fragility that she never displayed when awake.

In fact, she went out of her way to deflect any sign of emotion. Until last night.

After another bout of sensational sex, we'd talked long into the night. Corny stuff, like our favorite flicks and TV shows and childhood idols. I'd even done the unthinkable and turned off my mobile, something I never did, just so I could devote all my attention to Dani.

Because that's another thing I noticed. Dani seemed to thrive with attention. It's like she was starved of it as a kid and was making up for lost time now. Fine by me. I'd be happy to pay her all the attention she deserved for the time we had left.

That's when it hit me. I'd been so distracted, so captivated, by my new relationship with Dani I hadn't turned my mobile back on last night. It shouldn't be a problem but it was my only connection to Mum and I worried if the special accommodation couldn't contact me in an emergency.

Feeling a tad guilty, I slipped out of bed, pulled on jeans, and padded into the lounge room where I'd left it last night. I found it under a cushion, one of many that we'd pulled off the sofa when we'd gone at it the first time and hadn't made it to the bedroom.

I pressed the on switch and waited, knowing I'd have the usual messages from recalcitrant students wanting to reschedule their tutoring sessions and not much else.

But when the screen flickered to life, I had three messages from the special accom, thirty minutes apart, starting at six thirty this morning.

Shit.

Dread curdled in my gut as I spoke to the charge nurse, who outlined what had happened in succinct detail. Mum had wandered in the early hours this morning and had fallen, spraining her ankle, breaking several ribs and slicing open her hand so badly it needed stitches.

She'd been transferred to the nearest hospital and was asking for me. Fuck.

After disconnecting, I scrambled around for my clothes. I hadn't imagined the nurse's judgmental tone when they hadn't been able to contact me and I didn't blame her.

I blamed myself.

"You're not staying for breakfast?" Dani propped in the lounge room doorway, sleep-tousled and bleary-eyed, stifling a yawn. "I thought we could stroll down to Lygon Street for coffee and—"

"I have to go," I almost shouted, shoving papers on the coffee table aside in search of my wallet. "Mum's in the hospital."

"Is she okay—"

"I don't fucking know."

She flinched and rather than feel guilty, I felt annoyed. And incredibly angry that I'd been distracted to the point of stupidity last night.

"I'll call you later—"

"I'll be busy with Mum," I said, snatching up my wallet

and trying to ignore the heavy metal band jamming inside my head. "See you."

I ran out the door and sprinted for the nearest tram.

If only I could out-sprint my guilt as easily.

I'd really screwed up last night. I should never have turned off my phone and allowed myself to get distracted. And rather than accepting the blame, I'd pushed Dani away.

What a fucking mess.

For now, I'd see if Mum was okay and I'd deal with groveling to Dani later.

TWENTY-ONE
DANI

After Ash left, I went through the motions. Showered. Dressed. Ate cereal. But once I'd rinsed my bowl, stacked the dishwasher, headed into the lounge to watch some mindless TV and caught sight of the cushions scattered across the floor, the reality of what had happened came crashing down.

Ash and I had been so hot for each other last night we'd tumbled from the sofa to the floor along with those cushions. We'd been oblivious to everything, caught up in our newly created fantasy world where mismatched couples like us actually had a chance at happily ever after.

What a frikking joke.

It had been inevitable, Ash pushing me away. It was only a matter of time. It was what people did to me.

So it happened earlier than expected? Like twelve hours after I'd finally opened my heart to the possibility of a relationship. Shouldn't surprise me. It hadn't in the past and it wouldn't in the future.

But unlike those times in the past—when Mom didn't show for my grade school ballet concert, when Dad played a round of golf rather than attend my baseball tryouts, when Mia blew me off to spend the evening with Kye—this time the pain was so deep it gutted. I felt like my insides had been stabbed, diced and extricated one bit at a time, until all that was left was hollow.

I didn't want to feel like this. But I was done trying to obliterate my messes by using short-term memory swiping techniques.

Not once, in the last three years, had I forgotten. No matter what I tried, the memory was there. Taunting me. Haunting me.

A loud sob exploded from deep within and I collapsed onto the sofa, curled up in a ball, and rocked until I could breathe again.

I would survive this. I'd survived worse.

Then why did I feel like I was shattering from the inside out, one tiny piece at a time?

TWENTY-TWO
ASHTON

Thankfully, Mum was lucid when I arrived at the hospital. And despite three cracked ribs, a sprained ankle and a bandaged hand that had required nine stitches, she was in good spirits.

"Sorry I wasn't here for you last night, Mum."

She waved away my apology with her good hand. "Don't be silly. You can't be at the beck and call of a clumsy old woman day and night."

"But I had my phone turned off—"

"You have a life, Ashton." She smiled, the clarity of her eyes bringing a lump to my throat. "You need to live it."

"I do ..." Didn't I? Because apart from the wonderful times with Dani since she'd run me over, I hadn't been *alive*. Not really. I'd been functioning. Doing what had to be done. Playing the devoted son, working my arse off, at the expense of the things I loved. Movies. Footy. Painting.

I missed that most, the freedom to enter my studio and indulge in a creative free-for-all. Paint without deadlines, without constrictions. Paint for me.

"The nurses say you visit me twice a week," she said, patting the side of the bed for me to sit. "Is that true?"

I nodded and sat. "I'd come daily if I could but work keeps me busy—"

"I want you to stop." She held up her hand and it shook. "I'm sorry, Son. I love you. I've always loved you. But I can count the number of times I remember you coming to visit me in the last few months on one hand."

Her voice, which had once been so clear and vibrant, trembled with uncertainty. "I hate this bloody disease for that alone, that the one person in this world I adore visits and I can't remember. But that's exactly why I'm going to say this—"

"Mum, it's okay. I don't mind that you don't know me. It's part of the dementia and—"

"Stop. Listen." She stared at the bed sheets for an interminable time and I could see her lips moving slightly, as if she were rehearsing what she had to say. "Whether you come every day or once a year, I won't know. Am I happy I'm having a good day today? Bloody oath. But we both know it won't last and that as I deteriorate, there'll be more bad days than good."

Wow, during all the chats we'd had while Mum was okay and coming to terms with her dementia, not once had she been so accepting.

She held out her hand to me. "I want you to make me a promise."

I took her hand and squeezed. "Anything."

"Promise me you'll live your life on your terms. Take advantage of every opportunity that comes your way. Go away for a while. Take a holiday. Do whatever it takes to make you happy and don't feel guilty about me, okay?"

She was asking the impossible. As if I could go away

anywhere let alone on a holiday when she was in this state. Look what happened last night when I'd been off the grid for a few hours.

"Promise me, Ashton." Her tone had risen and rather than get her worked up, I nodded.

"Promise."

She raised my hand to her cheek and pressed against it. "You always were a good boy. My pride and joy."

"You're pretty amazing too, Mum."

Tears filled her eyes as she opened her arms to me. "Come and give your old mum a hug."

I didn't need to be asked twice as Mum gave me something more precious than her pep talk; a real, honest to goodness hug, the kind she used to give me as a kid. Tight, warm, squishy, with just the right amount of pressure.

Lord, how I missed her. I missed the woman she'd been every single day. Bright and bubbly and vivacious. Grabbing life by the throat and giving it a good shake up.

But she was right. I'd put my life on hold long enough. Meeting Dani, opening myself to the possibility of a relationship, had shown me I could have it all.

If she'd still have me, that is.

I'd behaved appallingly, courtesy of a raging hangover and bad news and my own guilt.

I needed to make amends, to show Dani exactly how much she meant to me.

And I knew just the way to do it.

TWENTY-THREE
DANI

"Thanks for coming." Ashton held out his hand to me.

I ignored it.

When he'd texted me an address and asked me to meet him here, I'd done it for one reason only.

Closure.

I didn't want the hurt of having my heart broken by Ash to fester the way it had after I'd lost the baby. It wasn't healthy and I'd finally realized that after three years.

Ironic, that it had taken another emotional breakdown to make me move on from the first. Not that I'd ever forget my baby and what I'd done, but opening myself up to the possibility of being loved, then having it taken away, proved I could do this. I could be strong. And I didn't need to forget, using whatever means possible. I merely needed to accept. Get closure. Move on.

"Why did you want me to meet you here?" I glanced at the brick cottage, a small part of me curious.

"I'll show you." He pushed open the rickety gate and gestured me to step through.

When I did, we headed along the cracked concrete

driveway to the back yard, where a detached room-cum-shed was tucked away behind the garage.

"This was my home, where I grew up," he said, pointing to the main house while he unlocked the shed. "We sold it years ago to help pay Mum's special accommodation bills, but I still rent this room from the owner."

"Why?"

He jiggled the door handle and opened the door. "Because of this."

I ignored my body's traitorous reaction, the familiar zap followed by a slow burning heat, as I pushed past him into the room. And blinked.

It took a while for my eyes to adjust from the bright sunshine outside to the dimness of the room, but when they did ... wow.

I did a slow three-sixty, unable to assimilate the brilliance of color, form and artistic license all at once.

"These are yours?" I murmured out of reverence for the stunning talent displayed in visual splendor.

"Yeah. This is where I come to paint. For me." He closed the door and flicked a light switch that merely enhanced his incredible work. "I don't get the time to come here often."

"You should make the time." I walked around the room, lingering in front of a particularly striking piece that looked like one of the laneways we'd visited. "These are amazing."

"Thanks." He cleared his throat. "You're opinion means a lot but that's not why I brought you here."

Just like that, I was back to the real world. A world where I had to face my demons and let others go.

"Look, you don't have to say anything, Ash—"

"I've never brought anyone here. Ever. Because all this?" He swept his arm wide. "It comes from in here." He tapped his chest. "Painting has been my outlet for years. The more I paint, the better I feel. And this place has always been my sanctuary."

He pinched the bridge of his nose, before pinning me with a tortured stare. "I over-reacted this morning and I'm sorry. I'm not used to having anyone else in my life and I felt guilty for having a good time and not being there for Mum."

He blew out a long breath. "But she'll always be ill. She'll only get worse. And putting my life on hold isn't going to change that."

He was so caring, so eloquent, so in touch with his feelings that it only made losing him all the harder.

"I'm sorry about your Mom."

"Thanks, but even though I freaked out this morning, seeing her today put things into perspective." He took a step toward me. "I don't let anyone get close, because it's easier that way." He pointed to my favorite painting, the one of the laneway. "That's part of a series I want to complete. It's my passion. Before you …"

I compressed my lips to refrain from responding because I sensed he had more to say.

"But I don't get here often because I need to pay Mum's bills, so when I'm not tutoring, I paint commissions." He grimaced. "I hate it but I want Mum to get the best care."

Admirable. And explained the half-finished canvases.

"You're an amazing son," I said, unable to identify with the love he had for his mom considering I hardly saw mine even when we'd lived in the same house.

"She's an amazing mum." He took another step closer and I held my breath at his nearness. "She made me see today I've had my life on hold and I'm not doing that anymore."

He snagged one of my hands before I could react. "Being with you has inspired me to finish this series. But considering how bloody time poor I am, I don't want my painting here to cut into our time together." His lop-sided smile drove the knife in my heart deeper. "So I want you with me. Here. Sharing my life."

He hesitated, cleared his throat. "I'm clueless when it comes to feelings but I think I'm in love with you."

I couldn't speak. Couldn't feel. Couldn't hear past the pounding of my heart in my ears.

Ash couldn't love me, because if he knew the real me, he'd despise me.

His smile faded when I didn't respond. "Say something, before I hit myself over the head with an easel or get high on paint fumes."

Get high ...

I couldn't prevent an embarrassing sob. Then another. And then I couldn't stop, each sob louder than the rest as I burst into tears.

"Hey." He bundled me into his arms and I let him, for the simple reason if he wasn't holding me, I'd be in a pathetic heap on the floor.

Because all those tears I'd bottled up for so long? Chose now to flow in a constant, ugly, snot-clogging stream I couldn't stop if I wanted to.

Ash smoothed my back, my hair, murmuring platitudes I couldn't hear. But it helped and eventually, the waterfalls cascading from my eyes dried to a trickle.

He eased me back, cupped my face, the tenderness radiating from his eyes making me want to bawl all over again. "You could've just said you didn't love me back."

I managed a wobbly smile at his joke. "You can't love me." I pushed his hands away, even though he resisted at first. "I do bad things."

Wariness crept into expression. "How bad can it be?

Because honestly? Nothing you can say will stop me loving you. And trying to make this work, despite the obvious barriers like distance."

Increasingly animated, he reached for me again. "Because I can visit you in LA. We can do long distance. Or you could transfer to finish your studies here permanently—"

"Stop!" My scream startled us both and he stilled, his hands falling uselessly to his sides.

"You want to know how bad I am?" My chuckle was harsh, brittle, and devoid of humor. "My parents spent their lives ignoring me, to the point they didn't know I got pregnant at eighteen. They didn't know I wanted the baby because it'd be the only person in my life to actually pay me some goddamned attention. They didn't know how badly I wanted to go to DU with my best friend, or how having to give that up stung, so I went out and got wasted, slept with a stranger, and ended up miscarrying the next day."

My voice had risen to the point of hysteria but like the tears, I couldn't stop it. "I killed my baby. My stupid selfishness killed my baby. And I've spent the last three years trying to forget by getting high whatever means I can or getting drunk or sleeping around."

I sniggered. "So how could someone as good and caring and straitlaced as you possibly love a self-absorbed slut like me?"

To my horror, tears filled Ash's eyes. "I'm so sorry you had to go through all that alone. I wish I could've been there for you."

My mouth gaped open. "What the fuck? Didn't you just hear a word I said? Aren't you disgusted?"

I turned away, rubbing my chest. Yeah, like that would stop the pain that had lodged there three years ago and never eased no matter what I did. "Because I certainly am. I hate what I've done and who I've become ..."

When he touched my shoulder, I whirled back and pushed him away. "And I can't stop. My new start in Melbourne? My do-over? A big fucking failure because old habits die-hard. My grades are shot. I'm drinking again. And I was this close" —I held up my thumb and forefinger an inch apart— "to scoring a hit the other day."

He didn't bat an eyelid, didn't move. "Why didn't you?"

"Because ..."

What could I say? Because I didn't want to be that person anymore? Because I wanted to make amends for fucking up?

"My best friend Skyped at the time. She talked me down."

"You still could've scored after the call. So what really stopped you?"

I sneered. "What are you, a frikking shrink?"

"I'm just the guy who loves you. And when you stop trying to push me away for fear you'll get hurt or lose me, you'll realize that," he said, his calmness both reassuring and annoying.

Didn't anything rattle him?

"Why do you love me?" I flung it out there in defiance, daring him to say something I could use as proof he was delusional.

"Because from the first moment we met, I sensed a kindred spirit." He pointed to my eyes. "You had this haunted look, like you had secrets." He shrugged. "And I did too."

He touched my arm. "But guess what, babe? All the secrets are out in the open now and we're still here. Doesn't that tell you something?"

Yeah, that I was bat-shit crazy for letting him talk me into this. But he was right. Ash now knew all my deepest, darkest secrets. He hadn't judged me or berated me or pitied me.

He still loved me regardless. Guess that's the moment I knew we could be okay after all.

"You said you think you're in love with me?"

He nodded. "Damn straight."

"Well I know I'm in love with you." I flung myself at him and he caught me.

Just like I knew this strong, dependable, incredible guy would continue to catch me for as long as we were together.

TWENTY-FOUR

ASHTON

Five minutes until show time.

I felt physically sick.

"You did good." Dani sidled up to me and kissed my cheek. "You're going to be the toast of the LA art world."

"Or laughed out of the country," I said, sliding my arm around her waist. "And I'll have you to thank for that."

She patted my cheek. "You're welcome."

I loved the teasing that was part of our yearlong relationship but now wasn't the time for frivolity. Now was the time for a few stiff drinks, for ignoring the throng of people queued outside the upscale Santa Monica gallery, and for strangling my gorgeous girlfriend for organizing my first official show.

"Seriously, babe. What if the US crowd don't get my paintings? What if this is a big, fucking failure?"

She rolled her eyes. "Sweetie, you know there's only room for one big fucking failure in our relationship and that title was held by me." She pinched my arse. "Before I met you, that is."

She threw her arms wide. "This laneway series you've

done? It's pure perfection and the art world will soon know it." This time, she tempered her arse pinch with a pat. "Trust me. I know a good thing when I see it."

"True, you're with me." I swooped for a quick kiss that never failed to set my blood fizzing. "And I thank my lucky stars you decided to stay in Melbourne to continue your degree."

She smirked. "It was the amazing Italian food in Lygon Street that swayed me. And the funky boutiques in Brunswick Street. Not to mention—"

"My charm? My wit? My status as resident sex god?"

"You forgot modesty." She whacked me playfully on the chest. "Just remember me when you're famous, okay?"

"You're unforgettable," I murmured, nuzzling her neck in the spot guaranteed to make her melt.

"Get a room, you two," Mia said, slugging us both on the arm. "Your public displays of affection are disgusting."

Dani laughed. "You should know, considering how you and your Aussie are still going at it."

Kye raised his hand. "Uh. Right here, in case you hadn't noticed."

"Oh, we noticed." Mia practically simpered as she cuddled up to her man. "Aren't Aussie guys the hottest?"

"Agreed," Dani said, batting her eyelashes at me.

Annabelle snorted and pretended to stick two fingers down her throat. "I've lived with them my whole life and let me tell you, Mia and Dani, you're a kangaroo short in the top paddock." She made crazy circles at her temple. "Aussie guys are rough, uncultured bogans." She flashed a grin at Kye and me. "Present company excluded."

We laughed.

"Maybe we should find you a hot Californian guy,

Annabelle?" Mia said, locking gazes with Dani, who gave a slight nod.

I groaned. "Watch out, Annabelle. These two are colluding to fix you up."

Annabelle shrugged. "Let them try. What's the worst that can happen?"

Dani and Mia sniggered, while Kye rolled his eyes, and I silently thanked the big guy upstairs.

Over the last twelve months, my relationship with Dani had gone from strength to strength. She'd settled in Melbourne, had passed all her subjects and had encouraged me to finish my laneway series. Not only that, through her parents she'd arranged my first showing here in LA. And had introduced me to her friends, who we'd hung out with over the last fortnight.

I'd even come to terms with Mum's deterioration. There was rarely a day she recognized me now and while it broke my heart and always would, I adhered to the promise I'd made her on the day I'd finally let love into my heart again.

A waiter appeared and handed us champagne flutes.

Dani raised her glass. "A toast to the most talented artist I know. May everyone love your wonderful art as much as I do."

"Hear, hear," Mia, Kye and Annabelle said in unison, as we clinked glasses.

"And to the woman I love." I touched my glass to Dani's. "Thanks for being you. I'm so proud of how successful you are in everything you do."

Dani teared up, I cleared my throat and the others groaned as I kissed her.

Something I intended on doing for a very long time to come.

Read Annabelle's story BLURRING THE LINE now!

ANNABELLE CLEARY TRAVELS *half way around the world...to fall in love with the boy next door all over again.*

Completing her degree at a college in Denver may just be the most exciting thing this small town girl has ever done. Until she discovers her new mentor is Joel Goodes, the guy who once rocked her world.

Joel isn't a keeper. He'll break her heart again. But Annabelle can't resist the sexy Aussie at his devastating best and soon they're indulging in an all-too-brief fling.

Annabelle wants it all: career, relationship and kids, in the hometown she's always loved. The same town that holds nothing but bad memories for Joel.

When they return to Australia, will it be a homecoming they'll never forget?

FREE BOOK AND MORE

SIGN UP TO NICOLA'S NEWSLETTER for a free book!

Read Nicola's newest feel-good romance **DID NOT FINISH**

Or her new gothic **THE RETREAT**

Try the **CARTWRIGHT BROTHERS** duo

FASCINATION

PERFECTION

The **WORKPLACE LIAISONS** duo

THE BOSS

THE CEO

Try the **BASHFUL BRIDES** series

NOT THE MARRYING KIND

NOT THE ROMANTIC KIND

NOT THE DARING KIND

NOT THE DATING KIND

The **CREATIVE IN LOVE** series

THE GRUMPY GUY

THE SHY GUY

THE GOOD GUY

Try the **BOMBSHELLS** series

BEFORE (FREE!)

BRASH

BLUSH

BOLD

BAD

BOMBSHELLS BOXED SET

The **WORLD APART** series

WALKING THE LINE (FREE!)

CROSSING THE LINE

TOWING THE LINE

BLURRING THE LINE

WORLD APART BOXED SET

The **HOT ISLAND NIGHTS** duo

WICKED NIGHTS

WANTON NIGHTS

The **BOLLYWOOD BILLIONAIRES** series

FAKING IT

MAKING IT

The **LOOKING FOR LOVE** series

LUCKY LOVE

CRAZY LOVE

SAPPHIRES ARE A GUY'S BEST FRIEND

THE SECOND CHANCE GUY

Check out Nicola's website for a full list of her books.

And read her other romances as Nikki North.

'MILLIONAIRE IN THE CITY' series.

LUCKY

COCKY

CRAZY

FANCY

FLIRTY

FOLLY

MADLY

Check out the **ESCAPE WITH ME** series.

DATE ME

LOVE ME

DARE ME

TRUST ME

FORGIVE ME

Try the **LAW BREAKER** series
THE DEAL MAKER
THE CONTRACT BREAKER

EXCERPT FROM BLURRING THE LINE

Annabelle's story.

Annabelle Cleary travels half way around the world...to fall in love with the boy next door all over again.

Completing her degree at a college in Denver may just be the most exciting thing this small town girl has ever done. Until she discovers her new mentor is Joel Goodes, the guy who once rocked her world.

Joel isn't a keeper. He'll break her heart again. But Annabelle can't resist the sexy Aussie at his devastating best and soon they're indulging in an all-too-brief fling.

Annabelle wants it all: career, relationship and kids, in the hometown she's always loved. The same town that holds nothing but bad memories for Joel.

When they return to Australia, will it be a homecoming they'll never forget?

ANNABELLE

Being an Aussie studying in Denver was cool. Unless your BFFs were dating hot Aussie guys and never let up on your lack of a boyfriend.

"I don't get it." Mia handed me a champers, as I thanked the gods I'd had the smarts to come to the States in my final year of uni so I could drink legally at the ripe old age of twenty-two. "You've been here a year, Annabelle, and you haven't hooked up."

Dani snorted. "Not that I blame her. Half the guys on this campus have a pole stuck so far up their asses they can hardly walk."

"Maybe she's too picky?" Mia topped up Dani's glass. "She needs to lighten up."

Dani sniggered. "And get laid."

I sipped at my champagne, content to let Mia and Dani debate my lack of male companionship. They'd been doing it the last three weeks, ever since opening night of Ashton's first art show.

Dani never shut up about Ashton, her sensitive-soul artist boyfriend. The fact she'd met him in Melbourne, while staying in my flat, kinda irked a little. During my three years doing a bachelor's degree in physiotherapy at Melbourne Uni, I'd never met a single guy I'd drool over the way Dani did with Ash.

As for Mia, she was just as pathetic with Kye, her sexy tennis jock boyfriend. With both guys being Aussie, it merely exacerbated Mia and Dani's relentless assessment of my less than stellar love life.

"How do you know I haven't hooked up or gotten laid?"

Mia clinked her glass with mine. "Because, dear friend, all you ever do is study. You don't date. You don't party."

"And you don't even consider Mia's fix-ups," Dani said, raising her glass. "Or so I've been told."

"How can I put this politely?" I finished my champers in three gulps before glaring at them. "Piss off."

Dani laughed. "I know for a fact that's the Aussie version of fuck off."

Some of the mischief faded from Mia's eyes. "You know we're only teasing?"

I nodded. "Yeah, but since the arrival of this one—" I pointed at Dani, "—you haven't let up."

Mia made a zipping motion over her lips at Dani, who was the more relentless of the two. "That's because we want you to be happy."

"I am." The quick response sounded hollow even to my ears.

Because the truth was, I wasn't happy. Sure, my studies were going great and I'd made a bunch of new friends while in Denver. But I missed Melbourne. And on a deeper level, I missed Uppity-Doo, the small country town in northern Victoria I called home.

If I was completely honest, the last time I'd been truly happy was back there, in my final year of high school, when the guy I'd adored had reciprocated my feelings on that one, fateful night I hadn't been able to forgot. Several years and a trip across the Pacific hadn't dimmed the memory. Sadly, no guy had come close to eliciting the same spark.

"Sure you are," Dani said. "You could almost convince us looking like this—" She pulled a face with downturned mouth and deep frown, "—translates to happiness in Australia." She rolled her eyes. "But I've lived there for the last twelve months, remember, and I happen to know that's bullshit."

Mia took the empty champagne glass out of my hand and draped an arm across my shoulders. "Listen, sweetie, we'll lay off if you promise to keep an open mind tonight."

"What's on tonight?" Like I had to ask. Yet another party where my well-meaning friends would try to foist some unsuspecting guy on me. A guy I'd chat with and laugh with while pretending to enjoy myself, knowing by the end of the night I'd be heading back to my dorm alone.

I wasn't interested in transient flings. Never had been. And with an expiration date on my studies here in the States, it was the main reason I'd remained single by choice.

The other reason, where I was pathetically, ridiculously hung up over a guy who didn't know I existed these days, was one I preferred to ignore.

"A few of us are heading out to that new bar in town." Mia squeezed my shoulders. "Apparently there's an Aussie guy in town Kye thought you might like to meet—"

"Not interested." I held up my hand. Yeah, like that would stop these two in full matchmaking mode. "Aussie guys are footy-loving, cricket-watching, beer-swilling bogans."

"We beg to differ." Dani smirked. "The Aussie guys we know are sexy, sweet and incredibly talented in bed."

"Hear, hear," Mia said, removing her arm from my shoulders to give Dani a high-five.

"You two are pathetic." I smiled, despite a pang of loneliness making me yearn for what they'd found with Kye and Ashton. "And for your information, I'm not going."

"That's what you think," Dani said, a second before she and Mia gang-tackled me.

We tumbled to the floor amid shrieks of laughter and hair pulling.

"Get off me." I elbowed Dani hard and followed up with a well-aimed kick to Mia's shin.

"Crazy bitch," Dani said, chuckling as she sat up and

rubbed her midriff, while Mia inspected her shin. "As if a few well-aimed jabs will get you out of going tonight."

Secretly admiring their determination to avoid me turning into a hermit, I folded my arms. "You can't make me."

"Want to make a bet?" Mia smirked. "If you don't want to come for social reasons, maybe we can appeal to your professional side."

Confused, I said, "What's that supposed to mean?"

"Apparently Kye met this guy when his shoulder tendonitis flared up today." Mia's smugness made fingers of premonition strum the back of my neck. "He's a physical therapist."

No way. It couldn't be.

"What's his name?" I aimed for casual, hoping the nerves making my stomach flip-flop wouldn't affect my voice.

Mia shrugged. "No idea."

"You'll just have to come to the bar and find out," Dani said, oblivious to the rampant adrenalin flooding my system, making me want to flee.

I was being ridiculous. There were many Australian physiotherapists working around the world. The odds of this Aussie physio being Joel were a million to one.

But that didn't stop my hands from giving a betraying quiver as I snagged my long hair that had come loose in our wrestling match and twisted it into a top-knot.

"We won't take no for an answer." Mia and Dani stood next to each other, shoulders squared, determination making their eyes glitter.

"Fine, you win." I held up my hands in resignation as they did a victory jig.

"You won't regret it, sweetie," Mia said.

I already did. Because if this Aussie physio was Joel Goodes, the guy who'd broken my heart, I was in trouble. Big trouble.

JOEL

I'd had a shit of a day.

Back to back patients for eight hours straight. Four meniscectomies, three rotator cuff tears, two carpel tunnel syndromes, an Achilles tendon bursitis, ankylosing spondylitis, torticollis, Osgood-Schlatter's, synovial cyst, popliteal effusion and a hamstring tear, and that had just been the morning.

I usually thrived on the constant buzz of diagnosing and treating orthopedic injuries at the outpatient clinic I'd worked at in downtown Denver for the last three months. The manic pace suited me.

Not today. Today, I'd been too busy mulling over Mum's late night phone call to fully appreciate the varying conditions I'd treated.

Mum was considering retiring and wanted me to come home to run her practice. A good offer, if the practice had been situated anywhere but Uppity-Doo.

God, I hated that name. Hated what it stood for more. Staidness. Stability. Stifling. Small town fishbowl mentality with a healthy dose of outback narrow-mindedness. Not that Uppity-Doo was outback exactly. Situated close to the Victorian-New South Wales border, it was four hours from Melbourne. And a million miles from where I ever wanted to be.

I'd escaped the town as soon as I could. Did my physio bachelor's degree in Melbourne and had been travelling ever since. Four years on the road. Locum work from

London to LA, and many cities in between. Three months in one city was ideal, six months at a stretch.

I'd been enjoying my stint in Denver, until that phone call. Mum's bollocking, about how I'd skirted responsibility all these years, rankled. She needed someone to take over her practice. That someone couldn't be me.

So when my last patient of the day, an Aussie tennis player, had invited me to a bar with some of his mates tonight, I'd accepted. A few beers would take the edge off.

But it wouldn't eradicate the inevitable guilt that talking to Mum elicited. She sure knew how to ram the bamboo under my fingernails and hammer the buggers home. She'd been the same with Dad. And it had killed him in the end.

I entered the bar and made for the pool tables, where Kye Sheldon had said his group would be. Would be good to chat to a bunch of fellow Aussies. Not that I didn't appreciate the people I met on my travels, but nobody did laid-back humor like Aussies.

"Mate, good to see you." Kye appeared out of nowhere as I neared the tables and slapped me on the back. "Come meet the rest of the gang."

A boutique beer was thrust at me by a guy on my left. "Cheers, mate. I'm Ashton."

"Thanks." I raised the bottle in his direction. "Been in the States long?"

"About a month." Ashton pointed at Kye. "This bloke's practically a local though."

Kye grinned. "Can't tear myself away from the joint."

Ashton snorted. "That's because his girlfriend has his balls in her back pocket."

I laughed and Kye held up his hands in surrender. "Guilty as charged, and loving it."

These guys had an obvious camaraderie and I experienced a rare pang. Traveling continuously wasn't conductive to mateship and I missed having someone, anyone, I could rely on.

I'd had a good mate once, back in Uppity-Do. A mate I'd eventually lost contact with deliberately, because of what I'd done with his sister.

Man, Trevor would've killed me if he'd found out about Annabelle and me.

"You can talk." Kye pressed his thumb into Ashton's forehead. "Yep, my thumb fits perfectly into the permanent indentation Dani has left there."

Ashton clinked his beer bottle against Kye's. "I'm a schmuck in love and proud of it."

They turned to face me. "What about you, Joel? You seeing anyone?"

I shook my head. "I move around too much to maintain a relationship."

The flash of pity in their eyes surprised me. Usually guys in relationships envied my lifestyle. And freedom was enviable. Not being tied down to one woman, in one place, for all eternity. Dying a slow death.

Ashton nodded, thoughtful. "Relationships are hard work, without the added pressure of distance."

"Listen to you." Kye sniggered. "Next you'll be braiding our hair and painting our nails."

Ashton's eyes narrowed but he grinned. "Dani likes that I'm a SNAG."

"You're not a sensitive new age guy, you're a lapdog." Kye lowered his tone and leaned toward me. "He's an *artist*. That explains a lot."

In response, Ashton punched Kye on the arm. Considering the size of the tennis player's biceps I'd seen while treating his shoulder earlier today, he wouldn't feel a thing.

"Better than being a Neanderthal masquerading as a college student while playing tennis for fun." Ashton made inverted comma signs with his fingers when he said 'for fun' and smirked.

I chuckled. "You two are like an old married couple. Been mates for long?"

"A month," Kye said, which surprised me. Ashton had said he'd been in the States a month but from their obvious bond I'd assumed they'd known each other longer. "Our girlfriends are besties, so since Ashton came over with Dani for his first art show, we've been hanging around a lot."

Ashton raised his beer in Kye's direction. "But lucky for me, I'll be heading back to Melbourne in a few weeks, leaving this funny man behind."

"You'll miss me," Kye said, deadpan.

"Like a hole in the head," Ashton muttered, his amused gaze drawn to the door behind me. "Don't look now, Sheldon, but your balls just made an appearance."

Kye elbowed Ashton and the artist winced a little.

"About time the girls showed up," Kye said, waving. "Don't worry, mate, they've brought a friend so you won't feel like a third wheel."

Shit, this better not be some lame fix-up. I wanted to have a few beers to unwind, not feel compelled to make mindless small talk with some chick I wouldn't see after tonight.

"She's a real hottie, too," Ashton said, elbowing me. "Check her out."

I glanced over my shoulder, the epitome of casual, and froze.

Because I knew the petite redhead with the killer bod striding toward me. Knew her intimately. And damned if my cock didn't harden at the memory.

Annabelle Cleary. The only good thing to come out of Uppity-Doo. And one of the reasons I'd bolted as fast as I goddamned could from that shithole town.

Kye bumped me. "What do you think?"

I am so screwed.

READ THE REST NOW!

EXCERPT FROM BEFORE

If you enjoyed this book, check out my other New Adult contemporary romance **BEFORE**, available at all retailers **FREE**.

Good girls finish last? Screw that.

Being a small town girl isn't so bad. Unless Mom's the town joke and I've spent my entire life shying away from her flamboyance. College in Las Vegas should be so much cooler. But it's not. Bad things happen. Real bad.

So when my brother Reid offers me an all-expenses paid vacation to Australia for a month, I am so there. Discounting the deadly snakes on the outback cattle station, I should be safe.

Until I meet Jack.

Jack defines bad boy and then some. He's big, buffed, bronzed, and hotter than any guy I've ever met. His sexy Aussie accent makes me melt. And the guy can cook.

But he's my brother's new bestie and he lives on the other side of the world. There's no future for us.

Is there?

JESS

College was overrated. Seriously.

The dorm-hopping, frat-partying, alcohol-imbibing rumors were true. The part where I became a party animal, made a zillion BFFs and took UNLV by storm? Hadn't kicked in yet. I sucked as badly as a freshman at the University of Nevada, Las Vegas, as I had as a student at Hell High, my nickname for my old high school in Craye Canyon. Apparently once a geek, always a geek.

In two semesters I'd attended three frat parties, had drunk two vodkas, one rum and a watered down Long Island Iced Tea. And the only other bed I'd graced besides my own belonged to my roommate's dog, illegally smuggled in whenever she could. Yeah, chalk up permanent virginity status alongside geek. Embarrassing.

On the upside, I didn't live at home any more. One of the major incentives for busting my ass at high school to enroll at UNLV was the distance. UNVL was over an hour away from my hometown so I'd have to live on campus. Craye Canyon wasn't big enough for Mom and me.

Pity my foray into freedom hadn't lived up to expectations. I'd hoped to shed my good-girl image at college. Yet here I was, last day before summer break, still hanging out in the library. Worse? Still a virgin.

"Hey Jess, you're coming tonight, yeah?"

I glanced across at Dave, my study partner, and bit back my first response of 'I wish.' Somehow, I didn't think the serious bookworm would appreciate the innuendo.

"Think I'll give it a miss," I said, packing my satchel for the last time this semester.

I was free for the summer. Without plans. I couldn't head home, not with Mom in wedding planner frenzy mode. Summer was the busiest month for Nevada weddings and it seemed like every bridezilla in the state wanted Pam Harper to organize their wedding. Poor suckers.

"School's out, Geekette." Dave tweaked my nose. "Time to par-tay."

"That settles it." I elbowed him away. "No way am I going anywhere with a dork who says *par-tay*."

"Now you're just playing hard to get." Dave slung an arm across my shoulder, a friendly gesture I'd tolerated during our many study sessions together.

"Yeah, that's me, a regular babe juggling guys along with assignments." I rolled my eyes. "Besides, I've got plans tonight."

"What plans?" He snapped his fingers. "Quick, the truth, before you make up some crap."

"I haven't seen my cousin in a while, thought I'd hang out with her."

Truth was, my cousin Chantal worked nights as a dancer at the coolest burlesque venue on the Strip. But she had a great apartment I could hide out in to avoid the inevitable end of semester parties.

I didn't feel like getting drunk, stoned or laid. Not that I'd ever done any of those things before. That Geekette nickname Dave had bestowed on me last August when we both started our undergrad English major? Pathetically true.

"Come to the party with me for a while, then go hang with your cousin later."

When I opened my mouth to protest again, Dave pressed his finger against my lips. "Not talking no for an answer, got it?"

I didn't mind Dave's arm around my shoulder but having his finger against my mouth made me uncomfortable. We were friends. We hung out. Two loners who studied and grabbed the occasional meal. I wasn't remotely attracted to the six foot, reed-thin Mr. Average and I'd never picked up any vibes off him.

But there was something about the way he was looking at me, the way he was muscling in on my personal space, that had me edging away.

"I might see you there," I said, slinging my bag over my shoulder and accidentally on purpose bumping him out of the way in the process.

For a second I thought I glimpsed anger in his pale grey eyes before he blinked and I attributed it to the sunlight filtering through the library windows.

"Okay, catch you later."

I waited until Dave left, watching him lope between the tables and out the main library doors. I liked his easy-going nature, how he joked around without crossing the line. He'd never put the moves on me so the whole touchy-feely finger on the lips? Probably harmless and just me over-reacting to having a long, hot summer stretching ahead of me with not one freaking thing to do.

I needed to get a life.

Fast.

JACK

I was a man on a mission.

I needed a bourbon in one hand and a blonde in the other, not necessarily in that order. And the annual Onakie B&S Ball happily provided both.

I'd traveled a long, dusty three hundred miles to attend

the black tie Bachelor and Spinster ball in outback Queensland, along with ten thousand other revelers currently jammed into the arena.

Festivities—translated: consuming as much alcohol as humanly possible—had kicked off in the afternoon, gates to the ball opened at seven, which meant there were a lot of B&S's paired off already. Nothing like beer goggles for making a member of the opposite sex appear overly attractive.

I hadn't run into anyone I knew, which suited me just fine. No one from the Cooweer Homestead cattle station where I worked had made the long trek. Then again, considering I was the only twenty-year-old on the property, with the next youngest employee being forty-five, it didn't surprise me. Besides, I preferred it this way. A few hours out of my mundane life to cut free. Go wild. Get pissed. Shag some willing and able chick.

It may not be much, but after spending the last four months working my arse off at the cattle station as a cook, I needed to burn off a little steam.

"Hey handsome. Gotta light?" A thirty-something blonde with sun-wrinkles ringing her big blue eyes touched my forearm, waving a cigarette in her other hand at me.

I shook my head. "Sorry. Don't smoke."

"Too bad." She flung the cigarette away and stepped in closer. "Fancy a drink instead?"

"Got one, thanks." I raised my bourbon. "But don't let me stop you."

Not deterred by my offhand responses, she threaded her fingers through mine. "Let's go dance." She paused and sent me a loaded glance from beneath her lash extensions. "Down by the river."

Code for 'my Ute is parked at the farthest corner of the

compound so we can fuck our brains out and no one will hear.'

This is exactly what I'd wanted. A no-strings-attached quickie to alleviate the boredom. So why did the thought of having meaningless sex with a stranger suddenly sound so unappealing?

She stood on her tiptoes and whispered in my ear. "I give great head."

I wasn't too keen, but my cock wasn't so discerning. It stood to attention, straining to get at the brazen blonde.

Sensing my indecision, she tugged on my hand. "Come on."

Like any weak-minded guy who allowed the wrong head to dictate his actions, I fell into step beside her. We dodged a crammed dance floor where an international rock band blasted hard core. We pushed our way through wall-to-wall revelers drunk on booze and each other. We wound our way through Utes and 4WDs parked helter-skelter. We sidestepped couples writhing against each other in the dark.

It was nothing I hadn't seen before. In fact, in the four years since I'd run from the last foster home in Sydney and worked my away across the outback to far north Queensland, I'd attended several B&S balls like this. Lonely people from all walks of life hooking up for a night of raucous fun, endless drinking and faceless sex.

I was over it.

"Here we are." She paused at the last Ute in a haphazard row. I couldn't see its color in the dark but it had an impressive chrome bull bar that shimmered in the moonlight. "You up for it?"

Before I could respond, she had her hand on my cock and her mouth on mine.

I wanted sex. Looked like I was about to get it.

Her tongue dueled with mine, demanding and taunting, as she unzipped me.

I groaned when her hand wrapped around my cock and pulled me free. She squeezed and pulled, teasing me, before dropping to her knees.

The moment her mouth closed around my cock, I closed my eyes, savoring the suction. Just the right amount. No teeth. A skillful gliding action of her mouth that milked me in wet velvet.

She was right. She gave frigging great head.

My balls tightened in anticipation but she was good at this, because she knew the right moment to stop sucking, fish a foil packet out of her bra and roll a condom on me in the time it took for my lust-hazed brain to clear.

"Very nice." She licked her lips with a slow, deliberate sweep of her tongue, before pushing me backward so I was lying flat on my back on the tray of her Ute. "Bet you feel as good as you taste."

She hoisted up her black satin gown and straddled me, giving me a nice eyeful of Brazilian, which she proceeded to play with. Her finger circled her clit as she sank down on me with a moan that raised the hairs on my arms.

There was something incredibly sexy about an uninhibited older woman bouncing up and down on the end of my cock, so into it that I was nothing but an adjunct to her pleasure.

It didn't take long for either of us. She brought herself to orgasm as she slammed down on me at a frantic pace, impaling herself so hard I saw stars when I came. Though that could've literally been the stars clustered in the clear outback sky framed behind her.

"How old are you?" she said as she clambered off and

headed around the side of the Ute to the cabin, giving me time to take care of the condom and zip up.

"Twenty."

She glanced up from the side mirror where she was busy reapplying a vivid red lip-gloss. "That's great. I've always wanted to fuck a guy half my age."

She beamed like I'd just presented her with the best gift ever, while my gut twisted. Guess I was as good at judging women's ages as I was at making decisions about where my life was headed. Absolutely shithouse.

Was this really what I wanted? Working my arse off cooking for a bunch of non-appreciative pricks for months on end, then spending my down time screwing old chicks?

My life was officially down the crapper.

"Thanks," she said, patting my cheek. "I'm heading back to the ball. See you round."

Not if I could help it and it wasn't until she disappeared from view that I realized we hadn't even exchanged names.

Fuck.

There had to be more to life than this.

READ THE REST NOW FOR FREE!

ABOUT THE AUTHOR

USA TODAY bestselling and multi-award winning author Nicola Marsh writes page-turning fiction to keep you up all night.
She's published 80 books and sold 8 million copies worldwide.
She currently writes contemporary romance and domestic suspense.
She's also a Waldenbooks, Bookscan, Amazon, iBooks and Barnes & Noble bestseller, a RBY (Romantic Book of the Year) and National Readers' Choice Award winner, and a multi-finalist for a number of awards including the Romantic Times Reviewers' Choice Award, HOLT Medallion, Booksellers' Best, Golden Quill, Laurel Wreath, and More than Magic.
A physiotherapist for thirteen years, she now adores writing full time, raising her two dashing young heroes, sharing fine food with family and friends, and her favorite, curling up with a good book!